CRICKET MAN

ALSO BY
PHYLLIS REYNOLDS NAYLOR

SHILOH BOOKS
Shiloh
Shiloh Season
Saving Shiloh

THE ALICE BOOKS
Starting with Alice
Alice in Blunderland
Lovingly Alice
The Agony of Alice
Alice in Rapture, Sort of
Reluctantly Alice
All But Alice
Alice in April
Alice In-Between
Alice the Brave
Alice in Lace
Outrageously Alice
Achingly Alice
Alice on the Outside
The Grooming of Alice
Alice Alone
Simply Alice
Patiently Alice
Including Alice
Alice on Her Way
Alice in the Know
Dangerously Alice
Almost Alice

THE BERNIE MAGRUDER BOOKS
Bernie Magruder and the Case
  of the Big Stink

Bernie Magruder and the
  Disappearing Bodies
Bernie Magruder and the
  Haunted Hotel
Bernie Magruder and the
  Drive-thru Funeral Parlor
Bernie Magruder and the Bus
  Station Blowup
Bernie Magruder and the
  Pirate's Treasure
Bernie Magruder and the
  Parachute Peril
Bernie Magruder and the Bats
  in the Belfry

THE CAT PACK BOOKS
The Grand Escape
The Healing of Texas Jake
Carlotta's Kittens
Polo's Mother

THE YORK TRILOGY
Shadows on the Wall
Faces in the Water
Footprints at the Window

THE WITCH BOOKS
Witch's Sister
Witch Water
The Witch Herself
The Witch's Eye
Witch Weed
The Witch Returns

PICTURE BOOKS
King of the Playground
The Boy with the Helium Head
Old Sadie and the Christmas Bear
Keeping a Christmas Secret
Ducks Disappearing
I Can't Take You Anywhere
Sweet Strawberries
Please DO Feed the Bears

BOOKS FOR YOUNG READERS
Josie's Troubles
How Lazy Can You Get?
All Because I'm Older
Maudie in the Middle
One of the Third-Grade Thonkers
Roxie and the Hooligans

BOOKS FOR MIDDLE READERS
Walking Through the Dark
How I Came to Be a Writer
Eddie, Incorporated
The Solomon System
The Keeper
Beetles, Lightly Toasted
The Fear Place
Being Danny's Dog
Danny's Desert Rats
Walker's Crossing

BOOKS FOR OLDER READERS
A String of Chances
Night Cry
The Dark of the Tunnel
The Year of the Gopher
Send No Blessings
Ice
Sang Spell
Jade Green
Blizzard's Wake

CRICKET MAN

PHYLLIS REYNOLDS NAYLOR

ginee seo books
Atheneum Books for Young Readers
NEW YORK LONDON TORONTO SYDNEY

Atheneum Books for Young Readers
An imprint of Simon & Schuster Children's Publishing Division
1230 Avenue of the Americas, New York, New York 10020
This book is a work of fiction. Any references to historical events, real people, or real locales are used fictitiously. Other names, characters, places, and incidents are products of the author's imagination, and any resemblance to actual events or locales or persons, living or dead, is entirely coincidental.
Copyright © 2008 by Phyllis Reynolds Naylor
Book design by Krista Vossen
The text for this book is set in Albertina.
Manufactured in the United States of America
First Edition
10 9 8 7 6 5 4 3 2 1
Library of Congress Cataloging-in-Publication Data
Naylor, Phyllis Reynolds.
Cricket man / Phyllis Reynolds Naylor. — 1st ed.
p. cm.
"Ginee Seo books."
Summary: Thirteen-year-old Kenny secretly calls himself "Cricket Man" after a summer of rescuing creatures from his family's Bethesda, Maryland, pool, which gives him more self-confidence and an urge to be a hero, especially for his depressed sixteen-year-old neighbor, Jodie.
ISBN-13: 978-1-4169-4981-7
ISBN-10: 1-4169-4981-X
[1. Heroes—Fiction. 2. Neighbors—Fiction. 3. Family life—Maryland—Fiction. 4. Schools—Fiction. 5. Skateboarding—Fiction. 6. Pregnancy—Fiction. 7. Maryland—Fiction.] I. Title.
PZ7.N24Cri 2008
[Fic]—dc22
2008005889

For our grandsons,
Garrett and Beckett Naylor

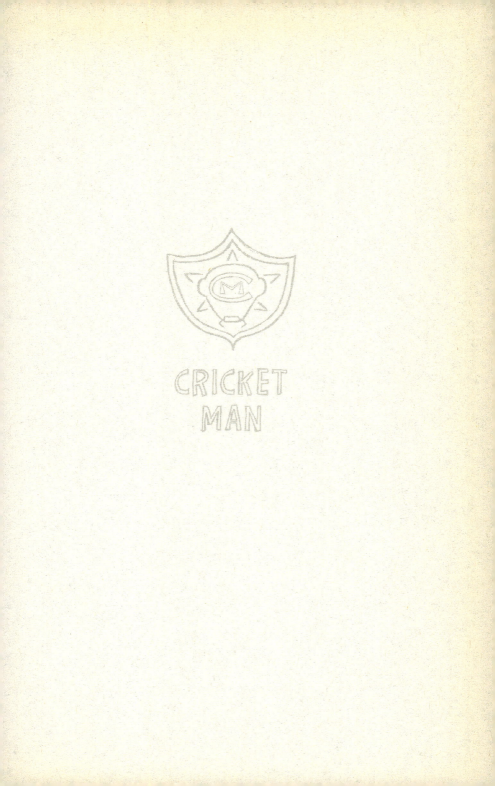

CRICKET
MAN

one

It's about midnight, I guess, when I see her on the roof of her porch.

There are four models of houses in our neighborhood, and every fourth house is like ours—two front bedrooms that look out over the porch roof, two back bedrooms. The minute Mom assigned me one of the front bedrooms, I knew I'd be out on the roof of that porch sometime. I knew I'd want to climb out there some soft spring evening. Sit out there some hot summer midnight. Some Saturday in fall, maybe—my ears a recorder, my eyes a camera—just watching the world.

Jodie Poindexter is at least three years older than me, and she's had a couple of different boyfriends since we moved here. She's in this big yellow house across the street, one house down, goes to high school, drives her dad's car, and has a complexion like peach ice cream. I go to middle school, don't have my license yet, and am currently sporting a couple of zits on my chin that look like I was stabbed by a fork.

There's something about being out on the porch roof at night that gives you a feeling of power. I mean, you know those signs? The ones with the human eye on them? WARNING: THIS AREA IS UNDER OBSERVATION BY A NEIGHBORHOOD WATCH PATROL? Well, I'm like that eye. I wear my navy blue sweats so I'm not too visible, and dream about the night I'll see a truck back up in a neighbor's driveway while the neighbor's away on vacation. Somebody will start hauling out TVs and computers and stuff, never knowing I'm there. It would be cool if I could swing down like Spider-Man and take out the bad guys. What would really happen is I'd crawl back in through the window and call the police.

Mostly, though, I just like to be out there to catch a breeze and think. What I think about most is school. Funny about middle school. You do one small thing out of line, and they notice—the kids, I mean.

There was this one girl, Mary Cerro, who had an accident in class. She got up from her seat and she'd bled on the back of her skirt. From then on, she was Bloody Mary. Not to her face, where she could have said something back. Guys just gave her mocking smiles, and after she'd pass, one would say, "Bloody Mary on the rocks," or something dumb like that. Like that one moment in time was going to define her forever.

And this guy Bill—Bill somebody. I don't remember because they moved away. But he stuttered. Mostly when he had to speak in class. He was a really nice kid—we ate together sometimes, talked about the Winter Olympics. He's a snowboarder. But one day in class he had to read his report, and he stuttered so bad he couldn't get past the first sentence. Kept blinking and tensing his jaw and we all felt . . . I don't know. Helpless. Like we wanted to do something but didn't know what. Even the teacher looked embarrassed.

Suddenly Bill started to cry. Quietly. Just stood there, tears running down his face, his neck and ears flaming red. The teacher said he could sit down, she'd accept a written report. I don't see how anyone in that room couldn't feel sorry for him right then. But the fact was that in those ten seconds between his last syllable and the crying, his eyes kept blinking and his head made little jerking motions. And later, someone called him Bill Blinky. The name stuck. From then on, he was known around school as "Blinky."

Middle school is where they never forgive. Or forget.

One time in sixth, I threw up in the library, and even though the janitor mopped it up, kids still walked around that spot on the carpet. "The Upchuck Kid," they called me, sometimes "Chuck" for short. They didn't know I swim. Didn't know I skate. You slip up once, buddy, you're done.

I've been in this new school now for a year, and am lucky, I guess. No label yet.

It's stuff like this I think about out on the roof, but this one night—I guess it's the first of August—I'm sitting out there in my invisible sweats. I'm leaning forward, arms resting on my knees, when I notice this person on the porch roof across the street, and she looks like she's naked.

Now I'm *really* staring. Then I see that she's got on a bikini. Or maybe it's just a bra and underwear. She probably doesn't realize that bare skin shows up pretty well in the moonlight. She's sitting on a towel or something, same position as me, arms resting on her knees, but her head's on her arms. Facedown. I mean, if you're going to go to the trouble to open your window, remove the screen, climb out with your beach towel, and sit on the porch roof, I'd think you'd sort of want to look around. Study the sky. But there she sits, Jodie Poindexter, with her head buried in her arms, and I wonder if she's okay.

I only see her around the neighborhood, so I don't know what she's like at high school. I just know that when our family moved here last September, she was going out with a tall, muscular guy. They broke up around Christmas, and after that it was a short, muscular guy who stopped by every morning to drive her to school in his dad's BMW.

Once I saw him bring her home around two in the morning. I was out on the roof that night. He parked down the block, away from the streetlight, and when they finally got out, he backed her up against the car and you could pretty much tell what they were doing. I figured she must like this guy a lot.

They went to the prom together in May. I watched Jodie, in her long black gown, come out of the house and get into this stretch limo with the row of lights along the side. But now, I realize, I haven't seen him around for the last week or so.

Sometimes you can tell by the shape of the shoulders if a person's sad. But this time I don't need shoulders to tell me. She shakes her head back and forth without even lifting it off her knees. Then she's still.

Whew! I'm thinking. I didn't expect this when I climbed out on the roof tonight. I hardly even know Jodie, and she doesn't know me. We're like two ships passing in the neighborhood night.

So I just sit there, watching her, and wish I could help. I wonder if she hears the crickets. A fire truck over on Democracy Boulevard. I hope she hasn't fallen asleep. If she has, I'll have to sit out here all night making sure she doesn't start to tilt. If she slumps over, I'll have to yell and wake her, so she won't fall off the roof.

But she isn't asleep. After a long, long while, she lifts her head and tips it back—way back—then hunches her shoulders about as high as they'll go and lets them drop.

She looks all around, and when she's turned in my direction, her head stops moving and I can feel my heart speeding up.

You can't see someone's eyes in the dark, but I just know—the way her body goes on alert—that she's seen me. Here we are, actually looking at each other.

I can't move. I can't even breathe. It's like we're each doing something we shouldn't, caught in a place we shouldn't be. For five seconds . . . ten, maybe . . . we just sit there in the moonlight, looking at each other. And then she stands up in her underwear, rolls up her towel, and—just before she crawls back inside—waves.

We've got a pool. There's no diving board or anything. Just this big rectangular hole in the ground. We have a blue vinyl liner, which is great if you bump the wall—no skinned elbow. But if we get a leak, I have to take a big breath and go under to patch it. Dad helps by holding me down with the skimmer pole so I won't keep bobbing back up. We're sort of primitive when it comes to pools.

"Omigod! We've got a house with a pool!" my sister told all her friends when Dad bought the house in Bethesda. That was last fall when I started seventh grade, which meant we wouldn't even be swimming till the following June. Moving around the beltway from Glen Burnie to Bethesda was no big deal for Marlene, because she's done with school—she's twenty—and can drive back to the old neighborhood whenever she wants.

Me? There wasn't any particular person I was sorry to leave.

"Hey, man! Maybe I'll see you around," one of the guys told me just before the moving van showed up.

"Yeah, maybe you can come over and swim sometime," I said, like anyone would circle the beltway just to swim in a pool that doesn't even have a deck around it—just a narrow sidewalk and a couple of chairs.

Davy was all for the move, though. He's like an open-faced sandwich—what you see is what you get. He's seven, and usually up for anything. You never have to guess what Davy's thinking; he'll tell you.

Dad bought a medical supply store in Bethesda, and Mom decided to take summer courses at the University of Maryland. She wants to get back into teaching. And this summer, because Marlene's working in the sportswear department at Macy's, Dad's paying me to take care of Davy when Mom's in class. I also have to keep the pool skimmed and vacuumed and mow the lawn. Seeing as how I can't get any other job till I'm fourteen, it's better than nothing. Bag the grass, chlorinate the pool, make a sandwich for Davy . . . If I had to write an essay for school, I'd call it "The Incredibly Boring Summer." And then one day I became . . . *Cricket Man.*

X X X

I swim pretty early in the mornings. Part of the deal is I have to be up by the time Mom and Dad and Marlene are leaving, so Davy won't go into the pool alone. And there's nothing that wakes you up faster than jumping in seventy-six-degree water in your shorts.

The thing about a pool in the early morning is that there are all these crickets and spiders and lightning bugs that fall in during the night. Some are already goners, floating upside down or lying on the bottom. The rest are like shipwrecked survivors, clinging to a leaf or twig. Mostly it's crickets. What I figure is that they make this blind leap from the concrete sidewalk, over the rubber coping at the edge of the pool, and—surprise!—land in the water. You have to admire their faith that there will be something solid for them when they land. Poor planning? Or no planning at all?

Then one morning I turn on the filter, as usual, and all the leaves and surface crud start moving slowly toward the little whirlpool in the skimmer box—all the June bugs and crickets and even a couple of honeybees, being drawn to certain death. And suddenly it comes to me: In the world of the cricket, I'm God. Only I can save them. Here are these helpless insects—they don't even know where they are—struggling madly against a riptide, and I, Kenny Harrison Sykes, will save them.

After that, I turn on the filter each morning and say,

"Okay, guys. Cricket Man is here!" And I swim around the whole pool, saving insects right and left. Sometimes I wait till the crickets are within inches of being sucked into the leaf trap, going faster and faster toward extinction in filter hell, and then . . . I put out my hand—a finger, even—like God and Adam touching in that Michelangelo painting—and the cricket latches on and I flick him to safety.

Once you fling it out of the water, though—once its life is saved—it doesn't jump or hop away and celebrate. It just sits there, stunned. Any bug will do that for a while. Maybe it'll twitch a leg. Tip a wing. What's it thinking? you wonder. Is it thinking at all? Does it realize how close it came? That it ought to plan that next leap? Probably not. Because sometimes, after I've used my superpowers to save it, it jumps right back in again.

Maybe, because I'm thinking about pools, I'm thinking about Jodie out on the roof in her bikini or underwear or whatever. Wondering again what was wrong. Wishing that I, Cricket Man, could save her. Help her, anyway. Even though we haven't said a single word to each other in the eleven months my family's been here. Until she waved at me the other night, Jodie and the crickets had one thing in common—they were all oblivious of me. If I held out my finger to a cricket, though, it would latch on out of desperation. If I held out a finger to Jodie, she'd probably say, "What are you *doing*?" and back away.

I'm not anybody's idea of God, of course, least of all an insect's. But I'm tall. I was probably the tallest guy in seventh grade last year. Tall and skinny, but with broad shoulders, decent arms. I've never had what you'd call a real girlfriend. First I have to figure them out, and that's taking longer than I'd thought.

There was this one girl, Ardyth, back in my old school. She asked her best friend to ask one of *my* friends if I liked her. She was sitting over on the swings watching me, but when I looked at her, she looked away. She was sort of cute, but she squinted a lot.

"I don't know," I said, and went on shooting baskets. My friend told her friend, and the next thing I knew, her friend tells my friend, who tells me that Ardyth's in the girls' room crying.

After the bell rang, I looked across the aisle at Ardyth's scrunched-up face and slipped her a note that said, "Okay. I like you." Because I felt sorry for her, see, and I figured if I wanted a girlfriend I had to start somewhere.

She read it and smiled and her face wasn't so scrunched up anymore, and I thought, *Whew! That's over. Now I've got a girlfriend and it's all settled.*

But at recess that afternoon, I'm over on the basketball court again and Ardyth's on the steps showing all the girls my note, like it's a trophy or something, and the girls are looking my way, giggling. And when the bell rings, her friends march across the playground like an army and tell me I'm supposed to hold Ardyth's hand as we go inside. When school's out, Ardyth asks me what time I'm going to call her.

"What about?" I ask.

"What do you think?" Ardyth says.

"I don't know," I tell her. Why was I supposed to call her if I didn't have anything to say?

"Well, if you don't know, I'm not going to tell you," she says.

"What's that supposed to mean?" I ask.

"Are we girlfriend and boyfriend or not?" she snaps.

I look at her face all scrunched up again, her eyebrows coming together over the bridge of her nose. "We're not," I say, and walk away. The shortest romance in the history of Glen Burnie Elementary.

That's the extent of my so-called experience. My friend James has this sister, Nina, a year younger than me, who won't get off the phone when I call. James has to wrestle the phone away from her. I go over to see him and she's right in my face, giggling and teasing and trying to get my attention. She doesn't take her eyes off me, and I feel like I don't have any clothes on when I'm around Nina. I say as little to her as possible, but she never gives up. I'm just cautious with girls, that's all. I've got a sister, so I know just how careful you have to be.

I guess you could say I'm a guy who doesn't need to be with people 100 percent of the time. And except for the usual middle-school insults, kids don't really pick on me, probably because I'm so tall. Dad says my feet are like flippers, and he's right, because I can do the length of our pool in six strokes.

I've never been in serious trouble and I do okay in school, so my parents don't worry too much about me. Marlene, though—Mom and Dad are real upset because she quit college. She wants to stay at Macy's and save enough to open a shop—women's shoes and stuff. Dad says she won't get very far without college, which doesn't help, and Mom's trying to set an example by going back to school herself.

I happen to think that what Marlene really wants to do is marry the guy she met at work, the one she's been sleeping with, and Mom and Dad don't have a clue. When I'm a parent, I at least want to have a clue.

Anyway, in this pathetic summer before eighth grade, the highlight of each day is to rescue crickets in the swimming pool. I wouldn't call myself lonely, exactly. Some evenings I hang with a couple of friends, James and Luis, and there's always stuff to do with my family. But a girlfriend would be nice. A crew to hang out with would be nice. Saving a neighbor's house from robbers would be nice. Being a superhero would be nice, but it's not the kind of thing you tell your friends.

three

I get weekends off——from keeping an eye on Davy, anyway. There's a small park where I hang out sometimes, a few blocks from our house. You go through a church parking lot to get there, then a grove of trees, past some tennis courts to a little playground with a picnic table. It's close to the firehouse on Democracy Boulevard, and when the station gets a call, little kids try to get there in time to see the firemen scramble and the trucks leave.

But I go to the park for the paved turnaround by the playground. It's a dead-end street, and skaters like to hang out there. That's where I met James. Dad gave me a skateboard when we moved from Glen Burnie——a compensation present for having to leave the old neighborhood, I guess. So in those first few weeks in Bethesda, I'd been asking around where you could take your board.

The same two guys were there the first few times I showed up. We were all beginners, but at least they'd polished up some tricks. They'd made a kind of ramp, three feet high, out of earth they'd packed down tight, with a piece of plywood on it. The board wasn't nearly as wide as it needed to be, and it slipped and slid around, but it worked.

I'd sit at the picnic table, my skateboard on one knee, and watch. A respectful distance, you know. They'd ignore me; glance over once or twice but not say anything.

Once, when one guy's board flew over to where I was sitting, I grabbed it for him.

"Thanks," he said.

"I could get you a bigger piece of plywood," I told him.

He'd studied me for a moment, then shrugged. "Sure," he said, and went back to the ramp.

But later, when the guys took a break, the taller one said, "Wanna try it?"

Not with both of them watching, I didn't. But I just nodded, got on my board, and headed for the ramp. I went halfway up before falling on my butt.

I could tell that the guys were grinning, but at least they didn't laugh out loud. "Dude, you had any practice?" the tall one asked. He was even skinnier than me, and his pants almost fell off him when he rode.

"Nah," I said. "I just got this board as a present."

It didn't take them long to see that I didn't know what

I was doing, and they set about teaching me to do an ollie with the board still pressed to the bottom of my feet. I'd almost figured that one out for myself, but they refined it for me. I wanted to learn the kickflip, though, and watched the way the taller guy spun the board around three hundred and sixty degrees while he was in the air.

"Put your toe right there . . . about that screw there," the shorter guy said, pointing to the board. He was stocky, with black hair, even the trace of a mustache, though I could tell by his voice that he was younger than me.

I toppled off when I tried, but the first guy said, "Use your nose, it'll go higher. Rolling's easier. I'm James," he added, and nodded toward the other guy. "He's Luis."

"Kenny," I told them.

By the time I went home that first afternoon last fall, I was getting a feel for it. The next time I went back, I dragged a big slab of plywood that had been left in our garage by the previous owner. And the week after that, something even better: my sister's balance beam from gymnastics that we'd propped in one corner of our new garage along with our badminton poles. Marlene hadn't used it since fifth grade.

James really went for that balance beam. They both did, he and Luis. It was meant for beginners and stood a foot off the ground, with long horizontal feet at each end to keep it from tipping. James has dreams of going pro some day. I don't. When I think about a career, I think photographer. I

think *National Geographic*. Colonies of chimpanzees, maybe—
what's going on behind those dark eyes, staring out at me
from the page. *Saving* chimpanzees, maybe. Them and the
orangutans.

But trying to ollie up and land on the balance beam—
not only land, but grind the length and drop off the other
end—became James's goal in life. I let him take the balance
beam home with him for practice after that. He'd bring it
out whenever we wanted to use it.

What I think about when I ride the skateboard is control. Middle school, see, is like an ocean, but you don't even
ride the waves. You're swept up by the current, one swirling
mass of arms and legs tumbling down the halls together.
On a board, though, *you* call the shots. Your eyes, your
brain, your nerves, your muscles—your grip, your speed,
your spin, your curve . . . Whether you land on your feet or
your butt, it's all up to you.

The three of us went to the same middle school, we
discovered—Luis a year behind James and me—but mostly
we practiced there at the park. At school we hung with different guys—Luis with his own class, James with the bikers,
me with anyone I happened to sit with at lunch.

So here I am, the following summer, just coming back
from the park where our ramp has been extended to six
feet wide. I walk in the back door, sweat dripping off my
jawline, and find I'm already late for dinner. And the first

thing Marlene says to me when she looks up is, "Kenny, do you know what happened to my old balance beam?"

I yank a paper towel and blot my face and neck, studying Marlene through my fingers to see how mad she is. Not particularly, I figure.

"You're taking up gymnastics again?" I ask.

"She's getting *married!*" Davy crows.

"On a *balance beam?*" I say.

And Marlene laughs. "No. I just want to practice walking so that when I come down the aisle in four-inch heels, I won't fall over." And she holds out her left hand with a diamond the size of a pencil eraser on her ring finger.

"Wow," I say. "The guy with the beard?"

"Goatee," Marlene corrects me, frowning a little. "Owen wears a *goatee.*"

What I'm thinking is, *Shave it off, Owen.* What I say is, "Well, congratulations!" I look at Mom and Dad to see how they feel about this. Hard to tell.

"When?" I ask, sticking my nose inside my shirt to see if I'm presentable enough to sit down at the table.

"They're talking about next spring or summer," Mom says, and she's smiling, so I guess she's okay with it.

"I'd really like to get married in April, but it will all depend on whether or not we can get the ballroom at the Oaks," Marlene says. "Owen and I would love to honeymoon in Paris."

"Well, if it's April, we certainly have to get busy," says Mom.

"We?" I say.

Marlene reaches across the table for a pickled beet, dangling it on the end of her fork. "Owen and I want to make it as easy on everyone as possible," she says to the rest of us. "But I'll want your input on everything." She puts the beet into her mouth.

Dad gives this sort of inaudible sigh you can sense by the way his chest rises, pauses, and falls. I've just begun to notice how deep the curved lines are on either side of his mouth, like parentheses, and the little vertical line on his forehead, just above his nose, like an exclamation point. You sort of find yourself waiting for the words that belong in those parentheses, so when Dad opens his mouth, you listen. But this time all he says is, "We don't have to get started this very minute, do we?"

Marlene laughs. "Of course not."

Dad smiles. "Then I just want to enjoy my coffee," he says.

Nobody brings up the balance beam after that, which is a good thing, because it's broken in two places.

On Sunday, Mr. Lambert, James's dad, drives us to downtown Bethesda when the office buildings are closed and picks us up a couple of hours later. There's this plaza with a sign on one of the pillars that reads NO BICYCLES,

SKATEBOARDS, ROLLERBLADES OR LOITERING ALLOWED, and it's perfect for skating as long as the security guard doesn't catch you. It's got two flights of five stairs each, plus handrails, so it's great for pulling off a trick, then rolling, setting up again, then landing and pretending you've nailed it.

James is a lot better at this stuff than Luis, and Luis is a lot better than me, but I'm gaining. At the Lamberts' house, James's whole room is Tony Hawk—posters and everything. He daydreams about going pro the way I daydream about taking pictures of an erupting volcano or climbing Mt. Everest or undressing Jodie Poindexter.

I guess I think about Jodie a lot since that night on the roof, wondering if she's okay. Once a girl lets you in on her feelings, even though she doesn't *know* she let you in on her feelings, even though you're not sure what those feelings really are, you can't let it drop. But when I see her again, I'm riding my bike past her house and I know she sees me because she's just going up on her porch. I *think* she turns around when I'm almost past, but I'm afraid I'll run into something if I look, so I don't look. And now I don't know if she said hi or not.

four

By the third week of August, I'm really bored with summer. Luis is off at some camp, James is away with his parents and sister, and all I hear at dinner is Marlene yakking on about her engagement. The wedding's been set for April 4. I'm running out of ideas for entertaining Davy. Not that I have to, but he's even more bored with summer than I am. The only good thing about Mom taking summer courses is that she's studying for finals, so we have takeout almost every night.

Dad brings Davy and me to his store one day to see the new sign up by the roof: SYKES MEDICAL SUPPLIES. Bold blue letters against a white background.

"Very professional-looking, Pops," I tell him, even though his store sits between a sub shop and a dry cleaner's on Rockville Pike. Dad's pleased that I like it.

"I figured now's the time," he says as we follow him inside. "I decided to wait a year before I changed the name—let customers get a chance to know me." Davy and I have been here before, of course, but it hadn't quite sunk in that the business belongs to Dad.

You have to wonder sometimes why people choose the jobs they do. I mean, my dad could have bought a pizza parlor, right? A surfboard shop? We could be standing here surrounded by dozens of new bikes, or the sign over the door could have read DRUMS UNLIMITED. Instead I'm staring at rows of blood pressure monitors, elastic stockings, knee braces, and bedpans. Signs above each aisle read RESPIRATORY PRODUCTS, BACK SUPPORTS, and BATHROOM SAFETY AIDS. The latest models of wheelchairs line the wall near the office.

Davy looks around uncertainly, and it suddenly hits: "Do you have to be sick to come in here?" he asks.

Dad says, "No, but some people are. I help them get better." I figure that must be the payoff.

He introduces us to the two clerks who are working that day, and then gives Davy and me the job of opening boxes in the back room and restocking some of the shelves. He even lets me run the cash register for a while as he packs up a customer's order. I'm just worried that he might turn to me and say, "Well, Kenny, someday all this will be yours." He doesn't.

X X X

I like our pool best in the early morning. It's different then. There's a walnut tree at one end and a box elder at the other, so the water temperature doesn't get much above eighty. The sun doesn't hit it till nine or so, and if I slide in real quiet without making a splash, animals hardly know I'm there. I can glide right over to the edge where a rabbit's eating clover at the far end of the pool. It'll stop chewing for a moment, its dark round eye fastened on me, and then it'll go right on nibbling, and I'm only a floating head, a lily pad maybe, on the surface of the water. A catbird will hop along the fence, observing, but as long as I keep my arms still, I'm some aquatic animal, powerless to do it harm.

You can't fool a chipmunk, though. We've got one living in a hole by the box elder, and that critter is *fast*. "Wee Willie," we call him. Now you see him, now you don't. But I sure have fun with the neighborhood cats.

They're predators, you know, prowling around in the cool of the morning, looking for a mouse or baby robin or even Wee Willie to pounce on. Little do they realize that Cricket Man is watching. When I see one approaching our backyard, I hunker down low in the water, only my eyes and nose above the surface, and move along, hardly making a ripple.

We have a chain-link fence around our backyard, hidden

by shrubbery, all but the gate. The cat leaps up on the gate, then jumps down into our yard and slinks along, lifting its paws high in the damp grass. I'm waiting for the moment it sees movement in the pool—sees my head skimming along the surface.

Then . . . the cat goes on full alert. First it freezes, one paw in the air. Then it crouches down and slowly . . . slowly, its tail straight as a poker, belly low to the ground, it stalks me. Two steps more . . . pause . . . wait . . . Three steps more . . . pause . . . wait . . .

I move closer to the edge of the pool so the cat will think it can bag me. On it comes, body quivering. The pupils grow large, their darkness filling up the whole eye.

Sometimes I give out these soft little squeaks, like a wounded animal, and this makes the cat crazy. When it gets so close that all four legs are in the pounce position, when its muscles tremble, whiskers twitch, I suddenly rise up out of the water with this enormous *swoosh*, my arms bringing up a spray like angel wings, a roar coming from my chest.

"CRICKET MAN!" I bellow.

I guess this is as close as I'll ever get to seeing an electrified cat, not that I'd really want to.

It jumps three inches off the ground. Its tail is thick as a baseball bat, the fur on the back of its neck is standing straight up like a hairbrush, and I mean, that cat is out of there—a streak of gray across the backyard, a ball of blur up over the chain-link fence, and it's not until it's down on the other side that it pauses once and turns around, tail swishing, then makes a beeline for home.

Of course the woman in the house behind us looks out her kitchen window to see what the weirdo's doing next. She probably didn't even see the cat. Probably thinks I'm having a peaceful swim and the next moment I'm having a seizure, but I never bother explaining to her. You can wear yourself out having to explain to people all the time.

The crickets are jumping into the pool regularly now, like they're committing mass suicide. One morning I rescue not only eleven crickets, but a locust, two lightning bugs, a beetle, and a daddy longlegs—all of them rushing toward certain death in the skimmer box.

Sometimes when I reach out to save a bug, it'll try to get away from me. But when it feels the pull of the skimmer box, it must know it's either me or extinction, and it chooses Cricket Man, its last hope.

The worst, though, is finding a small animal in the pool. One day I go out and find a baby rabbit. I don't know how long he's been there, but he's too exhausted to struggle. I grab the skimmer pole and quietly fish him out. He just lies there on the grass, tiny heart pounding. I can see it through his skin.

I don't try to touch him or anything, because they say that wild rabbits scare real easy. You can scare a rabbit to death. I don't know how he can be more scared after falling in a pool, but I just back away and go over to sit on the steps. Finally he begins to move. He gets up and slowly hops away. Man, I feel great then.

Does he even realize how close he came to dying? I wonder. Does he realize it was me who saved him? Then I get this idea. Out of boredom, maybe, or just for fun, I decide to design an insignia for Cricket Man, sort of like the shield on Superman's costume. If it turns out okay, I might even get it transferred onto a T-shirt—use it for underwear.

I get out some drawing paper and a pencil, sit down at the dining-room table, and begin to sketch.

When Davy walks in later, I have the outline of a cricket's head, facing forward, with a big C encircling an M in the middle of the face. Two eyes and two feelers. Then I erase the feelers because that's a little too obvious, and then I erase the eyes. A logo has to be simple. Finally I'm left with the cricket's head, with bulges on either side where the eyes would be. I'll paint the shield a dull green, with a big brown C and a bright green M inside it.

"What'cha making?" Davy asks, putting one knee on the chair beside me.

"Oh, just something."

"What?"

I'm painting in the C. "What does it look like?"

Davy leans over the table to get a better look. "Letters," he says. "A C and an M. It looks like a merit badge."

"It's a shield," I say. "An insignia."

"What does it stand for?"

"It's secret. If I told you, I'd have to kill you."

Davy grins. "Um . . . cat and mouse?" he guesses.

"Hey, you're good! But no."

He frowns and thinks some more. "Car mechanic?"

"Not even close."

"Tell me, then."

"If I do, it's just between you and me. Got it?"

He nods.

"I mean it," I say, and give him my serious look. "You can't tell *any*one, Davy. You have to agree to that." I'd be toast if this ever got around school.

"Okay, I promise," he says, and puts one hand on his heart.

So then I tell him about the crickets and the lightning bugs and the rabbit I'd found in the pool. I tell him how, out there, I feel sort of like God, only I can't be God so I'm Cricket Man. And just for kicks, I'm making myself a T-shirt, but I'll never let anyone know that Kenny Harrison Sykes is Cricket Man, even if they pull out all my fingernails.

"I won't either," Davy promises solemnly. "Even if they pull out my toenails, too."

"Shake," I say, and we do.

five

"So what do you think?" Mom asks me on Sunday as the two of us are finishing breakfast. Davy and Marlene are still sleeping.

"About what?" I say. "The pancakes?" Mom is small, so the only time we can look straight across at each other is when we're sitting down.

"Marlene and Owen. The engagement," she says.

"Jeez, Mom. Do we have to talk about it at breakfast, too?"

She laughs. "Not if you don't want to. Pretty boring stuff, huh?"

"Yup," I say. "But if they like each other, I'm okay with it." Seriously, what I'm thinking is that when Marlene moves out, I'll get her room. Huge closet.

Mom's quiet as she chews her toast. Then she says, "She's only twenty."

"Twenty-one in September," I remind her.

"But I *so* wanted her to finish college. Once a girl gets married . . ."

"She could still work and go to night school."

"But *would* she? Babies come along, they buy a house. . . ."

"Not babies," I joke, but she ignores it.

"And then," she says, "time just glides by."

"You had babies. You have a house, and you're going to night school." I don't know why I'm defending Marlene. I love her because she's my sister, but if I had to rate how I *liked* her, on a scale of one to ten, I'd give her maybe a four.

"But I went to college first! I have a degree! All I need are a few education courses," Mom says. "Marlene will have nothing."

"She just wants to run a little shop, Mom. She doesn't need a degree for that."

Mom stares out the window a moment or two. "Oh, I know. And I suppose I should be grateful, because she's matured a lot since she met Owen." She turns again and studies me across the table. Laugh lines make crinkles at the corners of her eyes. "So break it to me gently," she says. "What are *you* planning to do with your life?"

"Do I have to decide right now?" I ask, sounding like Dad, who's up on the roof repairing shingles. I can hear his footsteps overhead. Mom doesn't like him up there, but Dad says if he falls off, he can have any wheelchair in the store.

"No, but you must have thought about it," says Mom. "I just like to check in with you from time to time. If you could press a button and be anything at all, *do* anything, what would it be?"

"Besides driving a Jaguar?"

"Seriously."

I double-check with myself before answering. The last time she asked me this I was in second grade. I think I said astronaut. I wonder if she'll believe me any more now than she did then.

"I'd like to be a *National Geographic* photographer," I say.

Mom's face brightens. "Really?"

"Yeah. I've been thinking about it for a while."

"Sounds great! Dangerous, though . . ."

"Exciting," I say. "And yes, I plan to go to college, if that's what you're really asking."

"I'm glad, and that's what I was asking," she says. "It's important."

I take my Cricket Man insignia to a T-shirt shop on Auburn Avenue. They tell me it would turn out better if the colors were brighter, but I say it doesn't matter, so they put it on a white T-shirt while I wait.

It actually comes out better than I'd thought. The C and the M show up really well. So does the shape of the head—the shield. The bulges for eyes on both sides are a little blurred—you can tell it's a homemade design—but it's cool. I like it. When it needs washing, I'll do it in the sink. I don't want Marlene coming across it in the laundry, holding it up by two fingers, and asking, "What's *this*?"

Couple of days before school begins, Davy starts getting stomachaches.

"What's he been eating while I was in class?" Mom asks me, even though her courses are over. "Not a lot of candy, has he?"

"We don't do candy," I say. "Turkey sandwiches, Campbell's soups, tuna, grapes . . ."

"Probably the grapes," says Dad. "Go easy on fruit."

"And no sodas," says Mom.

I mow the yard on Labor Day, watching out for the chipmunk. The first time I saw Wee Willie, I was cooling off on the back steps. I'd thought it was a rat hugging the ground, but then I saw the stripes. So I'm really careful now when I mow, and afterward, I watch for it while I drink my Coke.

But on this afternoon when I finish mowing, I take my drink and some *National Geographics* out on the front porch and cool off there. Couple of seconds later Davy comes out and sits down beside me.

"Hey, buddy, what's up?" I ask, suppressing a belch. I try to hide the Coke can, but it's too late. He reaches for it, and I pull away. "Mom doesn't want you drinking any more sodas," I say. "She thinks they're giving you stomachaches."

Davy plunks back against the glider, head bumping the metal frame. "She shouldn't make me go to school then," he says flatly.

I look down at him. "What's that got to do with anything?"

He doesn't answer right away. I take a furtive sip from the can, then drop my arm between the glider and the wicker chair.

Finally Davy says, "Did they ever stick your head in the toilet when you were in second grade?"

"No. Who told you that?"

"Cory and Tom. They said after you leave first grade, they stick your head in the toilet if you can't spell."

I slap the palm of my hand against my forehead. "Don't you know it's the job of all third graders to scare new second graders into wetting their pants?"

"Then they don't make you eat boogers if you can't do take-away?" he asks.

"Heck, no. Not even if you can't add. If anybody tries to make you . . ." I put up my hands and take a quick punch at the air. "Pow! Bop! Biff! Bang! You let 'em have it. Just like Superman."

He grins at me. "Cricket Man, too? Does he have special powers?"

"Sure. He doesn't even have to use his fists."

Out on the street, cars are passing from both directions now—families returning home from their Labor Day weekend. The weather's dry, sunny, and walnuts are dropping like crazy from a neighboring tree every few minutes. *Poing!* They hit the roof of a car. *Clunk!* They hit the curb. Squirrels are having a field day.

"Watch," I say to Davy. "I can feel my cricket sense starting to tingle." I hold my hands out in front of me and shake them a little. Davy giggles. "And now," I say, "I will *make* those cars stop for squirrels. Keep watching."

A car's coming and a squirrel obliges. It starts halfway across the street, then pauses.

"Hold it . . . hold it. . . ." I warn the car as it slows. A second squirrel darts into the street, chasing the first. "Slow down now," I say to the car. "Easy . . . Just crawl. . . ."

It slows. It crawls, and the two squirrels reach the other side and skitter up a tree.

Davy jabs me with his elbow. "*You* didn't do that!"

"No? Here comes another one. . . ."

This time the squirrel barely escapes with its life because the car doesn't slow. But I yell, "Saved!" anyway, and Davy punches me again and laughs.

After he goes inside, I thumb through the magazines. Ever since Mom and I'd had that talk over breakfast the week before, it begins to sink in that she believes me. *In* me. That she's actually talking to me about the possibility of my becoming a photographer for *National Geographic. Some* kind of magazine, anyway.

Up until then, I figured that nobody took anything I said very seriously. No more than when I'd said I wanted to be a fireman when I was three. But lately I've been thinking, *Why not?* I have to be *something.* I'm not afraid of heights, so I can climb. I'm a good swimmer, so I can dive. . . . When we took a vacation in the Rockies, my pictures came out best. "Better angles," Dad said. "Maybe we should leave all the camera work to you!"

I spend a long time over the photographs, as I always do with a *Geographic,* but this time I find myself paying attention to the photo credits, seeing which photographers I like best. How the action tells a story, the captions draw you in: *Blood streaks a blanket of snow where a freshly slaughtered pig . . . Grabbing the safe end to avoid the lethal tentacles . . . A worker returns to the fields only two hours after delivering her own baby. . . . Having dozed off, he wakens to find himself a few feet closer to the sheer drop-off. . . .*

Oh, man! I think. For every picture of a guy hanging off a precipice or elephants charging, there's a photographer risking his life.

I put down one magazine and reach for another when I see Jodie coming around the house across the street, cell phone to her ear. I see her lean against a tree, holding the phone with one hand, the other hand over her eyes. She looks pretty upset about something, which is maybe why she's taken the phone outdoors.

For a few moments she just listens. Then she thrusts out a hand, palm up, in a helpless gesture. Listens some more. Finally she grabs at her hair and turns slowly around in a complete circle, talking all the while. I think she's crying. I feel as though I'm witnessing something I'm not supposed to see even more than I wasn't supposed to see her on the roof in her underwear.

After a while she presses a button on her phone and lets her arm drop. And then she goes inside.

I don't move, but I want to. I want to zap myself across the street, burst through the door. Tell Jodie to give the word and I'll go after the person who's making her cry. I don't know anything about Jodie Poindexter except that she's pretty. She's popular. But there's something so lonely about her that I want to help. I just don't know how. And I don't know how to stop thinking about her.

SiX

The worst part about the first day of school is taking the bus. I can't wait till I'm in high school, because we live so close we can hear the announcer at football games. But middle school's too far to walk, so the kids in my neighborhood slouch toward the corner at 8:13 and try not to get there too early. Too late, and your dad has to drive you. That's worse.

The trick is to arrive about the time you hear the bus rumble up the street from Lone Oak. People start emerging from doorways or out from behind shrubbery. There may be only one or two kids you know that first day, because government families move around a lot, and we're right outside DC. So we stand five feet apart with our iPods and headphones and pretend we're blind.

It's okay to stand off by yourself at the bus stop, but

once you're onboard, you're supposed to high-five a couple of friends. If you sit alone, you're considered pathetic. Doing almost anything alone in eighth grade makes you pathetic.

"Hey!" a small guy says, holding up his hand for the slap. He tries to high-five every boy who gets on the bus. Nobody sits by him unless he has to. I feel sorry for him, so our palms connect, but I go to the back and sit beside James, the one guy I know.

"How's it going?" I say.

"I'm *dead*, man!" he tells me. He looks it too. "Could barely open my eyes this morning."

I haven't told anyone I've been getting up at seven all summer. Haven't told them about looking out for Davy, or that Marlene's engaged, or about the crickets and spiders and the young rabbit I'd rescued in the pool. Heck, I've told Davy more than I've told my friends. Now *that's* pathetic.

The most descriptive thing you could say about James is that his pants hang low. Real low. Other than that, his clothes are unremarkable. He's not a Goth, a nerd, a geek, a freak, a jock. . . . He wears shirts the color of mud, all thrown together—the kind of guy who, if he was in a police lineup, you wouldn't recognize because he looks like every other guy on the street. He's just got this one overriding ambition to skateboard for the rest of his life.

Luis could hardly be more different. When we see him

around school, he looks great. Think of the latest thing in shirts or pants or shoes. That's Luis. It's just the way he is—his family is. He puts on T-shirts when he hangs out with James and me, but he still looks like he stepped out of a magazine. The one big thing he shares with James is his love for the skateboard, only he's not as obsessed about it.

Me? I hang with James and Luis because they were the first two guys I made friends with when we moved to Bethesda. And you always need friends.

The first day of school, there's the usual security guard at the entrance, eyeing our backpacks, checking us out. Once we're settled down in class, his only job is to be there.

Life's weird, but school's worse. Sometimes when I'm sitting out on the school steps with a bunch of guys, I'll look around and wonder if anyone else feels the same way. Like even our jokes and grins are right off the assembly line— pure plastic. Yet we—I do, anyway—still go around feeling like a pretzel in a bowl of potato chips.

Halfway through the morning, a couple of Montgomery County police officers show up. They chat awhile with the security guard, then amble through the halls between classes, smiling at students, kidding around with some of us as we go to gym. Just regular guys in black uniforms, see, so if we have anything to report, we'll pick up the phone and let them in on it.

x x x

My teachers seem okay; there aren't any real duds among them. But our vice principal is a different story. We had a really good one last year, but he's on sick leave for the semester, so we're stuck with a substitute vice principal, Mr. Funkhouser.

Nobody with a name like Funkhouser should have to be a vice principal. Not even a substitute. By the end of the second day, kids are calling him Finkhouse, Farthouse, all the obvious names, and by the end of the second week, we've got him figured out.

Vice principals have to have a game plan, see—some goals for the year. Somebody's cousin had him once and said his three goals for that year were respect for teachers, physical fitness, and emergency preparedness. From what we can tell here at our school, his three issues are going to be safety, nutrition, and self-image, because he takes his lead from whatever appears in the *Washington Post*. A story about Los Cholos, a new teenage gang in Virginia, and he's looking for graffiti on our restroom walls. A 17 percent obesity rate among students? Out go the candy bars in the snack machine. That much we can handle. But not this, which happens the first day.

Five minutes into lunch period, he's walking through the cafeteria looking for any kid, male or female, unlucky enough to be eating alone.

Now if you don't want to find yourself sitting alone on the bus going to school, you absolutely don't want to sit alone in the cafeteria at lunchtime. Even though you may basically *enjoy* eating alone, you might as well have a sign on your back flashing LOSER. Mr. Funkhouser knows this, of course, so—smiling and kidding—he makes each loner get up and carry his tray to another table.

I suppose he figures that before cliques are formed, he can mix in all the shy kids, the awkward ones, and other kids will discover what great personalities they have. Man, what a sense of humor! We'll all be one big happy family before the month is out. What a great idea!

It's almost too embarrassing to watch. He squeezes one girl in at a table where the others have to scoot down to make room. When he sees there's an empty space across from James and me, he goes over to a heavy guy in an orange T-shirt who's sitting alone, pretending he doesn't see Mr. Funkhouser coming.

But Farthouse won't be ignored.

"Hup, hup, hup," he barks, imitating a staff sergeant. "These are your marching orders, private," he jokes. "That table over there." And he nods toward us.

The kid's face is probably as bright as his T-shirt. He gives our substitute vice principal an embarrassed smile and bends over his tray again, hoping he'll get the message. Instead, Farthouser picks up the guy's tray himself and carries it to the empty spot at our table. Orange T-shirt has no choice but to get up and come over. There are a couple of other guys at our table, and they smirk at each other and go on talking in low voices. But I feel for the guy.

"Like we're back in third grade, huh?" I say to him.

He just nods a little, takes another bite of his sandwich and another slurp of his drink, then leaves the rest on the tray and walks out.

I sort of want to hang on to the feeling that I'm not exactly the same guy inside that I seem at school, somebody right off the assembly line. So I start wearing the Cricket Man T-shirt under my other shirts once in a while. Just one of those little secrets that gives you a buzz.

"So how's it going?" Dad asks me one evening.

"What?"

"School. How are things?"

"Okay," I tell him. "The vice principal's insane, but I can live with that."

"Do you see any evidence of drugs at your school?" Mom wants to know.

I give her the look. Like if somebody's dealing drugs, he'd post his phone number.

She still doesn't get it. "What about gangs?" she asks.

I don't crack a smile. "Oh, sure. They stand outside the

restrooms and charge admission," I say, casually spreading ketchup on my meatloaf.

"*What?*" says Mom.

Davy's staring at me, so I wink and he relaxes.

"Mom," I say, "there's nothing at school I can't handle, okay?"

She sighs and studies me for a moment. Then she smiles. "Okay," she says. "I'll turn all my worries over to you."

"Then can we talk about something else?" asks Marlene. "My wedding, for example?"

She launches into a long discussion of whether bold-colored bridesmaids' dresses are appropriate for spring. I listen so politely it's disgusting, because I've decided I really want Marlene married. The minute their car leaves for the honeymoon, my stuff's in her closet.

seven

The public pools close after Labor Day, but the weather stays warm and dry for most of September, so Davy and I keep swimming. Now and then one of us sees the chipmunk, but by the time he says, "Look!" Wee Willie's down a hole.

James comes over on Saturday and the three of us swim, tossing balls into a floating basket. When a shot lands out of the pool, Davy goes after it, and then he does a cannonball.

We've been in the pool about an hour when Marlene comes out to tell us we have to leave; Dad's going to vacuum it. Then I remember she's giving this big engagement party in the evening.

I wipe one hand across my eyes. "What's to vacuum?" I ask, looking around. "There's hardly any dirt on the bottom, and anyway, it's going to be dark."

"I want it *clean,* Kenny! This is an *engagement* party," she says firmly. "And I want to mop up all the water around the edge."

"But isn't this a *pool* party? Isn't the edge going to get wet anyway?" I ask.

"Kenny, stop arguing with me," she says. "I want it to look nice. C'mon. Out! Out! Out!"

She and Mr. Funkhouser could be cousins.

Davy groans disappointedly, but I give Marlene a military salute, and James and I climb out.

The good thing about an engagement party is that I don't have to be there, but I can slip in and out of the kitchen and help myself to the platters of food waiting to go out to the picnic table.

On the other hand, not every pool deserves a party. It's not like we have this great deck with umbrella tables and an amazing grill off to one side, the kind you see on TV. What we've got is a small concrete patio with a picnic table on it, then a wide expanse of grass, and at the very back of the yard, a pool with a sidewalk around it. That's it.

Of course, Mom rented some folding chairs, and Marlene stuck tiki torches here and there. Once it gets dark, the pool looks okay, I guess, but I'm not sure anyone's going to use it. Most of the people arrive in street clothes.

Only two couples wear their swimsuits under their

clothes. The women undress and stand around having drinks first, and then they go over to the pool, and the guys join them. One of the women, the one in the red and black bikini, screams, "Oh my God, it's a slug! I stepped on a slug!" and she jumps into the water to wash off her foot.

People laugh and make their way across the wet grass to the pool to watch. I go too and see this six-inch slug with a couple of his buddies slithering across the narrow sidewalk to the edge of the pool, leaving silvery trails behind them in the moonlight.

Then the second woman discovers she's in the pool with a cricket, and *she* screams. Everyone laughs, but Marlene's upset.

"Those damn crickets," she whispers to me. "Kenny, could you take the skimmer pole and get them out?"

I fish out the crickets and get the slugs, too, while I'm at it. I carry them to the back fence and tip them over into a neighbor's yard. Too bad Cricket Man isn't called on to save the woman from a rabid fox. A psycho raccoon. As I turn back toward the house, I can see Jodie's window across the street. It's dark. I wonder if she's sitting there looking out. Watching me.

The next day Dad tells me to keep myself available the following Sunday because he's going to need help putting the cover on the pool. Davy and I want to hold that off as long as we can, but the leaves are coming down fast now. Every little breeze brings a shower of leaves from the box elder, and we have to keep cleaning out the skimmer box.

I go swimming every day after school, even though the temperature's dropping. The crickets seem to hop into the pool along with me. If I rescue one with the net, he'll hop back up the pole and into the pool again before I can even tip him out. I rescue two, and four more take their place. I wonder sometimes why I bother, but I just want them to have a chance.

On Friday I'm making myself a chocolate shake in the blender after school. I look out the kitchen window and see little ripples in the water where a walnut, probably, has dropped. The neighbor behind us has a black walnut tree that hangs over one corner of our pool.

Davy comes in then and wants to read to me from a book he brought home from second grade. I stretch out on the sofa and coach from the sidelines when he stumbles over a word. Finally we decide to go for a swim before dinner.

Three feet from the edge of the pool, I stop and my breath stops and my heart stops, because Wee Willie's floating motionless on the surface of the water.

"No!" I lunge forward and yank the skimmer pole off the fence. "Oh, no," I whisper again as I scoop up the tiny body in the net.

"What is it, a chipmunk?" Davy asks, coming up behind me. "It's not Wee Willie, is it?"

We're too late. The eyes are glassy, the body cold. With a weight in the pit of my stomach, I know that the ripples I'd seen earlier weren't from a walnut dropping, but from a thirsty chipmunk that probably lost its balance hanging over the side of the pool. I could have gone out to check. Just one short walk to the pool and I could have saved him.

Gently I tip the net and the chipmunk falls into the grass.

"Is he drowned?" Davy asks, his voice trembling.

"Yes," I say.

"Can't you bring him back?"

"No, Davy."

He looks at me almost angrily for a moment, then relents. "Not even Cricket Man could save him, huh?"

I don't answer. I go to the garage and get the shovel. I bury the chipmunk under the azalea bushes, trying not to think of the way he must have paddled around, trying to find something to hold on to till he'd worn himself out.

We cover the pool on Sunday, and the leaves and walnuts that collect on top sit there in the puddles or are blown away by the October wind. The crickets that hadn't drowned themselves in the pool are migrating to our garage, and they jump every which way when we take out the garbage.

Schoolwork's piling up, and I wish we went to school early and got off at two thirty, the way high school kids do. Instead, we don't get out till three thirty. Sometimes when I pass Jodie Poindexter's house, she's sitting on her porch, wrapped in a sweater. We don't say anything to each other.

I have this fear that I'll suddenly do something wild to get her attention. Swing from a tree and bellow, maybe. When I want to do something especially brilliant, I can be so stupid. Like the time back in sixth grade when I asked our prettiest teacher if she'd had a nice summer, forgetting that her husband had died in July.

But Jodie doesn't even look at me. Just stares down at her lap. And I imagine Cricket Man walking right up to her steps and saying, "Tell me what's wrong and I'll take care of it." I imagine Jodie breaking into tears, running blindly out into the street, and Cricket Man swooping her out of the path of a speeding car.

And though she still doesn't see me, doesn't talk, doesn't wave, I decide right then that somehow I'm going to save Jodie Poindexter. From something.

In the meantime, I'm concentrating on skating with Luis and James, mostly polishing my wheelies and ollies. James is improving a lot faster than me because he really keeps at it, but my thigh muscles—and calves—are getting stronger.

Thicker, too. Between the three of us, we have a dozen or more bumps and bruises.

Halfway through October, though, I can tic tac and ride fakie. What I want to nail down before the weather turns bad is the pop shove-it. James wants to do a 50-50 grind, where he ollies onto a curb or something and grinds the axles of both trucks along the edge. Grinding sounds cool, but it takes a lot of practice.

He calls me on Sunday to say he's heard of a great place to skate, but we'll need our bikes to get there. So we meet at the park near the fire station and follow James down Fernwood to Greentree, then Greentree out to where it dead-ends—utility company land or something.

There's this big, empty house set apart from its neighbors, very formal-looking but shabby, with a FOR SALE sign in the front yard. The house must have been on the market a long time, because it's been a while since anyone trimmed the bushes. A crazy kind of trim too, like the kind they do on a show poodle. Like the owners couldn't stand to see a bush look like a bush, or a dog look like a dog. It's got to be trimmed or shaved in places.

"There's supposed to be a great place for skating in back," says James. "C'mon."

He's got that right. The lawn in back is more like a formal garden—a stone patio right outside the peeling French doors, and five cement steps going down to a wide walkway that goes on forever. Halfway down that walk is another set of five steps, and fifty feet beyond that, it ends at a fountain, surrounded by a low wall.

There's no water in the fountain, of course, and weeds are growing up over the edge of the walkway. It's a skateboarder's dream.

"Wow!" I say.

"This is awesome!" says Luis.

We stand there dreaming of possibilities. Doing ollies off the steps; grinding down the low wall on either side. Even trying out rides against the high wall at the back of the property. I get this idea to bring Jodie Poindexter here sometime after I get good, and entertain her. Make her laugh. Show off, more like it. Stupid. It must be my Cricket Man T-shirt giving me delusions. I wear it all the time now. But this is definitely the best place I've ever seen to skate.

Except that we don't deserve it. The steps aren't very steep, yet I take a slam at the bottom, trying to clear all five steps. I know I'll get a hipper from that one. Luis tries to grind on the low wall and falls down the steps. And no matter how many times James tries to ollie up onto the rim of the fountain and down again, he has to bail.

"Crap," Luis says after a while. "We suck, you know? All this space, and we suck."

"Takes practice, man!" James says irritably. "You think we can just try something once or twice and nail it down?"

But that's exactly what we'd thought. We're all trying things we aren't ready for. We finally settle for just practicing our backside 180s, and we definitely forget trying out the vertical wall.

I'm just getting the feel of ollieing off a couple of steps when I suddenly look up and freeze right where I am, my skateboard rolling away from me. Because standing up there on the stone patio in front of the French doors are two police officers, and one of them motions to me.

eight

We pick up our boards and amble over toward the officers, going up one set of steps, then the next. They're standing up there on the stone patio like it's a throne or something, like they expect us to bow down on one knee when we get to the top.

"You guys know you shouldn't be here, right?" says the first cop, the pudgy one. He's looking at me, but James shrugs.

"We weren't hurting anything," James says. "We heard the house was empty."

The officer turns toward James. "Just because a house is empty doesn't give you the right to trespass."

The second cop says, "This is the third call we've had from neighbors complaining about skateboarders coming over here to practice."

"It's the first time we've been here!" James protests. "We only just heard." His voice is full of indignation.

I can't tell if the police believe him or not. They look at him, then at me. They look at Luis. He's nodding his head.

"Where do you guys live?" asks the first cop.

"Over near Greyswood," says James. He's not about to give his address.

The cop looks at me.

"Same," I say.

Luis tells them he lives off Bradley Boulevard, and that sort of tells the police his folks have money. We're not just skateboard scumbags. At least one of us is a wealthy skateboard scumbag.

"Well," one of them says after a while. "Take your boards and clear out. If you come here again, we'll take you in." He motions with his thumb. "Outta here."

We walk over to our bikes. It's important not to hurry because it's the one thing you can still control, but it can't be *too* slow or the cops will think you're taunting them. My baggy jeans make a *thwack, thwack* sound as I walk across the grass. I pick up my bike, slip the trucks of my board over the handlebars where I can hold on, and head out.

We figure the cops'll go around us and leave, but they don't. The car follows us slowly along the road, like the end car in a funeral procession. When we get back to Fernwood, Luis gives us a wave and turns right toward Bradley. James and I turn left. The police car turns left. Five miles an hour, right on our tail. We cross the overpass on the beltway, and when James turns left onto Greyswood, I turn right. I figure the police will go straight ahead toward Democracy Boulevard. I figure wrong. They follow me.

I swallow and my throat feels dry. What's going on? I'm the tallest, maybe, so they figure I'm the ringleader? Or they're ticked off I let James do the talking? But they tail me up the street where I make the turn. They make the turn. Humiliating me, that's what. They follow me all the way back to our house. And there in the driveway, getting out of his car, is Dad.

He starts to reach in the back for his jacket, then slowly straightens up and stares at me and the police car. I slow down to turn into the driveway. The police car slows down. I make the turn. The police car stops. I park my bike by the garage and glance toward the street. The cops, both of them, are just looking toward our house—at Dad and me— not saying a word. And then . . . slowly . . . they move on.

Dad looks at me. "What was *that* about?" he asks.

Screw them, I'm thinking. "Nothing," I say to Dad. "They were on our case for skating, but we weren't hurting any- thing." I start up the front steps.

"Hey!" he says, and I stop. "*Where*?"

"I don't know. An empty house with a big garden in back. Cement walks and stuff. Nobody there. We heard it was a great place to skate." I'm not looking at him when I answer. If the cops had wanted to make a big deal out of it, they would have gotten out and talked to Dad. They didn't, so that should be the end of it. Not with Dad.

"Who were you with? You alone?"

"James and Luis."

"What's Luis's last name?"

"Calderon."

He thinks a minute. "So why did the police follow *you* home?"

I shift impatiently. "I don't know, Dad. They just did. Maybe because I look like the oldest. They just warned us not to go back there."

"You sure that's all there is to this?"

I let out my breath. "Yes. If it was more than that, the cops would have talked to you. Right?"

"Well . . . probably." Dad reaches into the car and gets his jacket, then follows me into the house. He doesn't tell Mom. Chalk one up for Dad.

There's something that bothers me, though. Dad's *You sure that's all there is to this?* When did the police ever follow me home before? I wonder if he's going to look up "Calderon" in the phone book and check out Luis's family. *Jeez!*

A little privacy, that's all I'm asking. My parents worry about everything. Then I'm thinking, do Jodie Poindexter's parents worry about her? Maybe they should. But both of them are lawyers, I've heard, and they're gone all day, so how would they even know that she sits over there and cries?

Halloween falls on a Friday this year, and the school decides to hold a party. We've never had one before, but this time the whole community's involved. Last year on Halloween, at another school, somebody got knifed. So the idea is to make us think we're having a good time but keep us safely locked inside till our parents come to pick us up. Marlene drives us over. Luis's parents won't let him come at all.

I have this fantasy of making a huge cricket head and coming to the Halloween party as Cricket Man. Of course I don't. James and I just go with ties around our necks—like a white-collar desk job is the weirdest costume yet—but a lot of kids come as dancers or singers or their favorite football players—how hard is it to wear a number twenty-six sweatshirt?—or they come in one of these corpse-looking rubber masks with their skin tinted green.

There's a lot of noise, a flashing strobe light, fortune-telling, video games, a miniature bowling alley, food, movies . . . everything necessary to keep us there. Once we go inside, there's a lockdown, and we can't get out till eleven.

James goes off to play the video games, and I'm looking for the dips and chips when this kid in a turban comes over and asks can I help him out for a minute.

"Sure," I say. He's one of the jocks, I think, so I'm surprised he's asking *me*.

"I have to read palms at the fortune-telling booth, but I've got to use the john. Take my place for a couple minutes?"

I open my mouth to say "Huh?" but he's already taking off the purple turban and popping it on my head.

"What do I have to do?" I croak.

"Just read palms," he says. "There's a chart. . . ." And he takes off.

The turban's tipping, and I straighten it up as I walk over to the booth and sit down at the card table. I'm under this tentlike thing with a lantern at the back, and sure enough, there's a diagram of a hand on the card table.

Some kids go by and grin at me. James sees me and doubles over.

"I'm just filling in for somebody," I tell him.

Five minutes later I begin to wonder if this guy's coming back, and ten minutes later I know he's not. I'm about to take off the turban when these two girls come by dressed like flappers from back in the 1920s. Short dresses, long beads, headbands.

"You go first," the brunette says to the blonde.

"No, *you*!" The blonde giggles and pushes her friend down in the chair across the table.

The brunette looks at me. "Are *you* Zircon the Great?" she asks skeptically.

I can feel the blood rising in my neck, my ears. "Uh . . . sort of."

"*Sort of?*" she says, extending her palm.

"Predict her love life," says the blonde, still giggling.

I see a guy coming by from my math class, and quick as a blink, I take off the turban and stick it on his head. "Zircon the Great," I say to the girls.

"Huh?" he says, but I'm outta there.

I feel sort of guilty, but I didn't ask to be Zircon. Couple of minutes later, though, I edge back just close enough to see what's happening, and the guy's still there with the turban on his head, only now the blonde's in the chair and he's checking out *her* palm.

"And *vat*, my lovely, do you vant to know?" the guy's saying, really playing it up, and the girls are going nuts over him.

I feel like an idiot. Why couldn't that have been me? How come *I* don't think of things like, "*And vat, my lovely, do you vant to know?*" I can think of really great stuff to say about a minute after I should have said it.

I move on across the gym to where some girls in hula skirts and bikini tops are dancing. There are three of them, and they're pretty good at it, except that every time they bump into one another, they break into giggles and stop dancing for a minute. Seventh graders, but cute. Heck, I wouldn't know how to talk to them, either.

Then I realize that one of them is Nina Lambert, James's little sister. She sees me, and the blood starts rising in my neck again. Great. Now I'm a stupid thermometer. "Hel . . . lo, Kenny!" she says, coming over and trying to put her Hawaiian leis around my neck. I stop her and give the leis back, my face fiery red as the other girls watch and giggle. I can't think of a thing to say, so I just keep walking. And I'm stuck in the gym till eleven o'clock.

nine

The day after Halloween is gorgeous, with a moon so full it's almost daylight. I do my homework, then settle down to read all the newspaper comics I've missed this week. I even read the incredibly dorky ones like *Mark Trail*. I really miss *The Far Side* and *Calvin and Hobbes,* and I wish Spidey would get his act together.

About midnight, I go up to bed. I lean over to turn on my lamp when my eye catches something white across the street. I crouch down at the window. It's Jodie Poindexter, wrapped in a blanket, sitting on the roof of her porch. My mouth goes dry and I can feel my own heartbeats. For a full minute or two I just watch her. She doesn't have her head buried in her arms this time. She's leaning back against the side of the house, the blanket covering everything but her face. I can't really see her expression.

And suddenly I'm taking off my navy shirt, stripping down to my Cricket Man tee. I'm yanking stuff out of my closet in the dark, looking for my khakis, my white socks, any light-colored clothes I own. I don't want to turn on my light. Don't want to catch her attention till I'm out there on the roof, bold as anything. She waved at me once, so I'll wave at her. I'll wave both arms like I'm sending her a message by semaphore. *Cricket Man's watching. Just call on me.*

I find my khakis but not my socks, so I'm barefoot. I yank a pillowcase off the bed, grab a white sweatshirt for my other hand, and pull open my window wide. Take out the screen. I crawl out on the roof, the grit of the shingles cold beneath my feet, and lift my arms to signal.

The roof across the street is empty. Jodie's gone inside.

James calls me Tuesday evening. "I found a great place to skate," he says.

"Yeah, right. You and your places."

"Really!"

I give him a chance. "They get that old skateboard park in Rockville repaired?"

"Not yet. But there's a place over in Silver Spring. The county's set up the lower level of a parking garage for skateboarders. It's only till they finish some construction out on the road, but it's worth a try."

"The whole lower level?"

"That's what I heard."

"How are we supposed to get there?"

"Mom's got a dentist appointment tomorrow at four. If you bring your board to school, she'll pick us up and drive us over."

"Boards aren't allowed at school."

"Yeah, so? Smuggle it in. Be creative. I'll call Luis," he says.

On Wednesday I try to fit my board into my gym bag, but the top sticks out. So I wrap it in plain brown paper, like a big loaf of French bread, then stuff it partway in.

Getting it into the school turns out to be no big deal. Crowds of kids are all coming in together. I've got my backpack over my shoulder, gym bag under my arm, and I'm laughing and messing around with James, who's left his board in his mom's car. The security guard's joking with a couple of girls and waves us through. I store my skateboard in my locker because I've got to take the gym bag down to PE.

"You good?" we ask Luis when we see him.

"Yep," he says. "Left my board under a bush."

"Meet us out at the side entrance after school," says James. "My mom'll pick us up there."

When I get to my locker at three thirty, though, I realize I left my bag in the gym. Luis and James are probably already out in the car. The girl at the locker next to mine must be having a birthday, because a bunch of balloons are tied to the handle. Three friends are standing there dividing a huge muffin with a candle on it.

I put on my jacket and glance at the girls. When I think they're not looking, I pull out my paper-wrapped skateboard. It clanks against my locker door, and the girls turn around. I try to tuck it under my arm, but it slides beneath my jacket instead, pokes way out in back. I can feel the breeze. *Real smooth, Kenny.* One of the girls looks at me and nudges the others. I get out as fast as I can. Just the weirdo at the locker next to you, ma'am, that's me.

I get to James's car. He's in the front seat beside his mom. I pull out my skateboard and crawl in back beside Luis.

"Hello, Kenny," Mrs. Lambert says. "I hope this place is worth it. A parking garage doesn't sound all that great to me."

"Depends," I say.

None of us ever says much when we're in a car with a parent. It's like anything we say is being recorded and transmitted to the other parents. There should be a big sign on the back of the front seat: YOU HAVE THE RIGHT TO REMAIN SILENT, AND ANYTHING YOU SAY MIGHT BE HELD AGAINST YOU. We play it safe.

When we get there, she lets us out. "Pick you up at five fifteen," she says. "Be here on this corner, James. Don't make me have to come looking for you."

We get out and go over to the parking garage, take the stairs to the lower level. There are already a few guys there—some girls, too—and that's embarrassing because they're all a lot better than we are. But the place is huge. We scope out one corner and head there.

Luis and I are just practicing some basics in the long empty stretch of the garage—the heelflip, the kickflip, the nosegrab, the wheel slide. James, though, is taking those concrete ridges at the front of each parking space one after the other. He ollies onto each one so that both trucks grind against it, then pops off and takes the next. Each of us falls down a time or two, and Luis skins a knee pretty good. Tears a hole in his jeans. But it feels great to be back on the boards again, and we give it all we've got.

The next day, first period's half over—Mr. Olson's discussing the Bill of Rights, and how many of us would sign it today if we didn't know what it was—when we hear the chimes that signal a message from the office.

"Sorry for the interruption, Mr. Olson," the secretary's saying, "but would you send Kenny Sykes to the office? Thank you."

Everyone looks at me.

"Kenny?" the teacher says, and nods toward the door. He waits, like he won't continue the lesson till I'm outta there, so I stuff my notebook into my backpack. I'm wondering what forms I didn't turn in at the office, what fee I haven't paid.

Out in the hall, I lope toward the office and go up to the desk.

"Kenny Sykes," I say.

"Yes, Kenny. Mr. Funkhouser wants to see you. Go on in," the secretary says.

What does Farthouse want with me? It can't be good. I walk over to the doorway and look in. He's reading a page from a file folder. I give a little knock, and he turns his head.

"Kenny?"

"Yeah."

"Come on in. Close the door, will you?"

Shit. I go in and drop my backpack on a chair, sit down on the other. My legs extend all the way under his desk.

"How you doing?" he asks.

Doing fine till you called me in, I want to say, but I don't. "Okay."

"I was just looking at your record, Kenny, and I see that you came to this school last year from Glen Burnie. Am I right?"

"Yeah," I say again.

He smiles. "So how's it going? Making friends?"

"I'm doing okay," I say. *Hey, I'm not sitting alone in the cafeteria,* I'm thinking. *What's the problem?*

Mr. Funkhouser leans back, elbows on the arms of his

chair, fingertips touching. "Having any problems we should talk about?"

"No," I say.

"Well, let me ask. Who are the people you hang out with most?"

Why's he so interested? What the heck? Now I can't even choose who I sit with?

"I know a lot of people," I say.

"Okay. Let me be more specific: Who were you with yesterday after school?"

Alarms are going off in my head. If I lie and say I was alone, it'll look like I'm trying to cover up for my friends. And if I name names, it'll get James and Luis mixed up in whatever nutty idea Funkhouser is hatching. But since we were in James's mother's car and have an alibi for whatever Funkhouser thinks we did, I figure we're okay. "James Lambert and Luis Calderon," I say. "Why?"

He writes it down and repeats the last names. "Lambert and Calderon."

"So what's this about?"

"I'm wondering what you were hiding under your jacket when you left the school." I stare. He's not smiling now. He's actually serious. "Several people reported suspicious behavior at your locker. They said you were hiding something long and metal under your jacket as you left school yesterday."

The birthday girls. It's all so ridiculous I don't even feel I have to answer. I give him a sarcastic smile. "An AK rifle, what else?"

I see his jaw tense. "I asked a serious question," he says.

"A skateboard," I tell him. "It was a skateboard."

"A skateboard," he repeats, like he hadn't heard the first time. "Why would you hide that under your jacket?"

"Because they're not allowed at school." *Duh.*

"James and Luis bring skateboards too?"

I shrug.

"Where did they keep theirs?" he asks.

"I don't know," I say. "We were just going to meet somewhere after school."

"Where?"

"A parking garage in Silver Spring."

"A parking garage? To skateboard?"

"Yeah. It's temporarily open for skaters."

He doesn't believe me, I can tell, but I don't care. *Asshole.*

"Who else did you meet in the parking garage?"

"Nobody."

"No one else was there?"

"There were a few other guys, but we didn't know them."

Now he's giving me the once-over, whether to believe me or not. He's staring at my chest. I look down. My denim shirt is open, and behind it you can see my Cricket Man T-shirt, the logo dead center.

"I'm curious about that shirt," says Funkhouser. "I'd guess it's a homemade design?"

"Yeah," I say, and feel my face start to color a bit.

"C . . . M . . . What does that stand for, Kenny? Just curious."

I can't believe this. There is no way in the world I'm going to sit here and tell Funkhouser about the pool and the crickets and the rabbit I saved and the chipmunk I didn't. No way I'm going to tell him about playing at being Cricket Man.

I look away.

"Kenny?" he asks.

I turn back again.

"What do those letters stand for?"

"I can't tell you that," I say.

ten

Funkhouser's face goes hard and cold. There are two little creases on either side of his mouth, and they get even deeper. "Why can't you tell me?"

Because it's stupid and childish and weird, I'm thinking. *You'd never in this world understand, and neither would the other kids if it got out.* "Because it's personal," I say.

He thinks about that a moment. Stops playing with his fingertips and rests his chin on his folded hands. Reminds me of the Irish setter we used to have, resting its head on its paws. "Then why are you wearing that shirt to school if it's so personal?" he asks.

My mouth is so dry my lips stick together. I hear myself saying, "My underwear's personal too, but I wear that to school." This is getting more ridiculous, but I think I'm as angry as I am scared. Up until now, I'd gotten along pretty well with most of my teachers, but Funkhauser stumps me.

His palms go flat on his desk as he straightens up. "Listen, Sykes, we do have regulations about what's appropriate at school . . . ," he's saying.

Can you believe this? I'm thinking. *What is the big deal?* It's a frigging Fruit of the Loom T-shirt! Ninety percent of the guys are wearing T-shirts with anything from death's-heads on them to BIKE NAKED, and I'm called into the office for *this?* I wouldn't tell him now what CM stands for if he set my fingernails on fire. My heart's pounding.

"And obviously," he continues, "there's a reason you're keeping those initials secret. Tell me this: Has anyone *told* you to keep them secret?"

He's insane. He's a raving lunatic.

"No!"

"You can go, Sykes," he says, as the bell rings, "but I don't want to see that shirt here in school again. Do you understand?"

I stare at him. My chest is about to explode.

"Is that understood?" he asks.

I shake my head. No *way* is he going to get away with this!

"I *said* I don't want to see that shirt here in school again. Go to your next class. We'll continue this another time."

I walk back through the office with blood rushing in my

temples, the throb of it sounding in my ears. Funkhouser has reached a new low. Now I want to wear my Cricket Man T-shirt to school every day as much as I've ever wanted anything. I am so right and he is so wrong!

By the end of the day, half the school has heard about what went on in Funkhauser's office. Everyone wants to know what CM stands for on my T-shirt.

It's Luis and James's fault. I hear all about it at lunchtime. After my session with the vice principal, he calls in James, then Luis, and asks each one of them separately if they'd brought their skateboards to school the day before. James says no, the truth. Luis lies and says no.

Then Funkhauser asks, did they go with me to a parking garage in Silver Spring? James says yes. Luis says yes. And then Funkhauser wants to know what the CM on my T-shirt stands for. James says, "How would I know?" and Luis says, "What T-shirt?" That's how much attention we pay to stuff like this. But Funkhauser thinks they're stalling. And afterward they go around telling everyone what a jerk Funkhauser is.

All day kids are grinning at me, giving me high fives, like I'm a celebrity or something. Everyone's playing the game:

"Cement Mixer?" they guess.

"Crazy Maniac?" they say.

I just smile and shrug them off, which makes the whole thing seem even more mysterious.

X X X

I get off the bus at the corner and walk the block and a half to my house. Inside, I can hear the TV going—Davy gets home about an hour before I do—and when I walk in the kitchen, Mom's sitting at the table, staring at me as I open the fridge. She's wearing her old green sweater, which she changes into as soon as she gets home from classes at the university.

"Kenny," she asks, "what in the world is going on between you and Mr. Funkhauser?"

Oh, crapo. I get out a carton of orange juice and go to the cupboard for a glass. "He's trying to make a federal case out of absolutely nothing," I say. "What'd he do? Call?"

"Of course he called! He left a message on the answering machine." Mom turns her hands over, palms up, clueless. "He wanted to know if you brought a skateboard to school yesterday, and I said I didn't know—that I hadn't seen you carrying one when you left. And then he said he was merely trying to get some information from you about what you'd been doing after school, but you weren't cooperating. Something about a *T-shirt?*"

"He's crazy, Mom. He needs help."

"Kenny, this is not funny. He didn't sound crazy to me. He sounded concerned," Mom says. "Did anything go on at that parking garage yesterday that I should know about?"

"No!" I'm practically shouting. "We were skating! I told

him that. What does he mean, I wasn't cooperating? Yeah, I took my skateboard to school because Mrs. Lambert picked us up after last period to drive us over. I'd wrapped it in paper to hide it, but that's not exactly a felony."

"Then what is Mr. Funkhauser so upset about? And what does the 'CM' stand for on the T-shirt he's talking about?"

"It's just something private," I say. "It doesn't concern the school and it's none of his business."

I reach for the crackers, then the peanut butter jar, but Mom catches my arm. She's looking straight at me. "So what do those letters mean?"

I don't answer.

"Kenny?"

There's hurt in her voice, and I hate that. I hate that she gets hurt so easy. I hate that Funkhauser made that stupid phone call and upset her over an incredibly idiotic thing like a homemade logo on a stupid T-shirt. *If it's so stupid*, the right hemisphere of my brain asks the left, *why don't you just tell her?*

And I'm thinking, *Because it's mine.* It's one of the few things that I can hold on to. That I own. It's a part of my imagination, stupid as it is, and that's a part of the private me.

"I'm sorry, Mom. I can't tell you," I say.

Mom drops her hands and they fall into her lap. "Kenny, what *is* it?" she asks.

"Mom, will you just forget it? Will you just *trust* me on this?"

The TV goes off in the other room, and Davy wanders into the kitchen. He starts to reach for the crackers, then looks at Mom. Looks at me. "What's the matter?" he asks.

"Nothing," I tell him.

It's like Mom doesn't even know he's there. "All I ask," she says evenly, "as your mother, is what 'CM' stands for. That's all I'm asking. I'm not going through your dresser drawers or listening in on your phone conversations or reading your mail."

"I appreciate that," I say, "but I *really* need you to trust me. Give me that little bit of privacy. *Please.*"

Mom doesn't answer.

I forget the crackers, pick up the orange juice, and start to leave the kitchen. Davy's eyes are wide. Excited. And behind Mom's back, he gives me the thumbs-up sign.

Every nerve in my body feels alive as I go upstairs, but my stomach's slightly sick. If I had to hurt Mom like this, why couldn't it be over something big? And yet, don't trust and respect count for anything?

Dad works late, but the next morning I can tell that Mom's told him about Funkhauser's message on the answering machine. He doesn't bring it up with me before school because he doesn't like arguments at breakfast. But I can see his eyes studying me over the box of cereal and the bagels.

"Kenny," he says, as he gets up and wipes his mouth, then drops the napkin in his cereal bowl. "Just take it easy today, huh? Try not to take life so seriously."

"Yeah," I tell him.

I'm wearing the T-shirt again, with a brown checked shirt over it. Kids grin at me, girls whisper. Smile.

I brace myself for another call to the office during homeroom. Doesn't happen. First period . . . second period . . . third . . . It's right after lunch, during math, that the speaker comes on in the classroom.

"Mrs. Stacy, sorry to interrupt, but would you send Kenny Sykes to the office, please? Thank you."

"Tell him 'Chunky Moose,'" someone says, and everyone laughs.

I smile a little, pick up my books and backpack, and head for the hall, then down the stairs to the first floor. I'm prepared for battle this time. I'm psyched.

I head for Funkhouser's door, not even looking at the secretary. She stops me.

"Wrong way," she says, pointing in the other direction. "Mr. Lawson's office."

Lawson? The school psychologist drops by our school twice a month. Mostly he does testing, but once in a while he has a private conference with a student—the kid who tried to set his jacket on fire, the tall girl who won't eat anything but fruit, the girl whose dad abused her, the guy whose family was killed in a car crash. And now, there's me and my *T-shirt*? This is too weird.

"You're kidding," I say to the secretary.

She gives me a funny but sympathetic smile. "I kid you not," she says. "Go ahead."

We skipped a step here, I'm thinking. First the vice principal, then the counselor, *then* the shrink. I think of demanding to see the counselor, but instead I open the door to Mr. Lawson's office and walk in.

A fortysomething man in a sport shirt looks up and smiles at me.

"Ah! The T-shirt!" he says. "Come on in."

eleven

"This is getting ridiculous," I say.

"Well, let's talk about it," Lawson says. I can see his eyes checking out my chest. "That the infamous T-shirt?" He's not at his desk. He's sitting in one of the two chairs across from it, where parents probably sit when they come for a conference. I slump down in the other, our feet practically touching.

I look toward the window, bored. Defiant. I can feel my heart beating faster.

"You design that yourself?" he finally asks.

"Yeah." I glance at Lawson for a second, then away again.

"So it's the C and the M that are in question?"

"Mr. Funkhouser is the only one who questions them," I tell him.

He nods. Another ten seconds go by. When I steal a look at him again, I think he's smiling. Then I'm not so sure.

"I went over your record, Kenny, and your grades are good," he says. "You've got a couple of detentions for cutting class, but nothing more serious than that. No problems with teachers. So what do you suppose Mr. Funkhouser is upset about?"

I pull back my feet, turn one sideways, and rest the other foot on top of it. Then I put both feet on the floor. "Because he can't stand that he doesn't have one hundred percent control over everyone when we're here at school. Because he's got to be a big shot and can't admit he went too far in telling me I can't wear this T-shirt."

Did I just say that?

He nods. "Okay. I'll accept your version. But let's play it over one more time. Two girls go to the office and report that you're acting secretive—I think that's the word he said they used—at your locker two days ago, and they noticed you were trying to hide something 'long and metal' under your jacket. Funkhouser calls you into the office the next day and you tell him it was a skateboard, which is not allowed here at school, and you make a joke about an AK rifle. He asks what you did after school, and you tell him you and two friends went to a parking garage where some other guys were hanging out."

"Jeez!" I say. "He should write for the movies."

This time the smile breaks through on Lawson's face, but he keeps going: "You tell him that all you guys were doing was skating, but when he happens to comment on your T-shirt—on what those letters stand for—you clam up and say you can't tell him. As though it's . . . well, an oath, perhaps, that you've taken never to tell."

"Wow," I say. "Let me know how the story comes out, okay?"

Lawson's serious again. "Kenny, whatever you might think of Mr. Funkhouser, he's our interim vice principal. It's his job to keep the students safe, and when there's suspicious activity, it's his job to investigate, no matter how trivial it may seem to you. There have been stories in the paper about a gang over in Virginia, and Mr. Funkhouser wants to be sure that the C on your T-shirt doesn't stand for Los Cholos."

I stare at him openmouthed.

"Does that surprise you?" he asks.

I have to laugh. "Nothing Funkhouser does could surprise me, but I'm amazed at his imagination," I say. "Do I look Hispanic?"

Lawson just cocks his head a little and continues, "So . . . here you are and here I am, and I have to ask, will you tell me what those letters *do* stand for?"

"As though if I were a member of Los Cholos I'd wear it on a *T-shirt*?" I croak, and hate that my voice breaks just then. "Like maybe 'CM' means I'm a Los Cholos Man?"

He waits.

"Well, it doesn't stand for that, but it's something personal," I say, more politely. Lawson leveled with me, and I owe him that. "And I can't believe that a stupid T-shirt with a homemade design not only gets me a private audience with the vice principal, but an emergency session with the school shrink as well."

But he's smiling now. "Actually, Paul and I were just shooting the breeze this morning, when I mentioned I had a testing cancellation today, and he asked if I could see you— just give him my take on what you were about. That's all there was to it."

I like Lawson. I believe him.

"So . . . ," he says, "I'd like to make a deal with you. I'll tell Mr. Funkhouser that we had our little talk and that I see no reason you can't continue wearing that T-shirt to school . . ."

I'm waiting for the catch.

". . . if you can assure me that there is nothing about that logo that is connected to a gang, that's derogatory toward any person or group, or that in any way could bring harm to our school."

"Yeah," I say. "I can guarantee that. And you can tell Funkhouser I wouldn't know a Los Cholos from a Chihuahua." Man, I'm on a roll!

His eyes look amused, and Lawson leans forward in his chair. "Okay, Kenny, thanks for coming in."

I blink. "That's all? That's it?"

"That's it," he says, and grabs the arms of his chair, ready to stand up.

I hear myself say, "Well, thanks." I pick up my backpack and turn toward the door.

"Oh, Kenny," he says, and I stop. "One more thing. Could we keep Mr. Funkhouser's suspicions just between the two of us? I'm going to trust you about the T-shirt, and I'd like to trust you on this."

I know right away that he doesn't want Funkhouser to look any worse than he already does. And I could spin off a story that would make him look like Fool of the Year. But I like that Lawson trusts me. "Yeah," I say. "I won't mention it. You can count on that."

"Thanks," Mr. Lawson says, and smiles. And I leave. Smiling.

It's weird and not so weird, this Cricket Man thing. Like it's starting to get larger than life. All I did was create something to play around with in my head when I'm in the pool, and suddenly it's got a mystique all its own. Stranger still, when I'm talking about CM with Lawson, I say things I would never have said to him before. To any adult before. I'm not so far gone I believe in special powers or anything.

It's just that when I'm defending my right to privacy, I'm braver than I thought. And maybe it's all coincidence that I'm wearing the T-shirt, but it's enough to give me a buzz.

I get off the bus that afternoon and walk the block and a half toward home. James has to buy some shoes, and Luis promised his folks he'd rake the yard, so I'm thinking of taking my skateboard over to the park and practicing alone. Work on my ollies. It's warm for November, and the sun's been out all day. Feels good on the back of my neck. I'm trying to remember just where James said to position your feet on the board when I hear somebody say, "Hi."

I glance around. Turn a little more.

Jodie Poindexter is sitting on her front steps. She's got a denim jacket draped over her shoulders, and she's smiling at me. I can't believe I was almost past her house and didn't see her.

"Hi!" I say, wondering. Is this the first time she's ever spoken to me?

"Hear you caused a commotion at your school yesterday."

I'm standing out there on the sidewalk, staring at her. "Who told you that?"

She grins. "My friend's sister is in eighth grade. She told us about it."

"Yeah," I say, embarrassed that she knows. "It blew over, though. No big deal."

"Wanna sit down for a minute?" she says, motioning to the steps.

Do I want to sit down with Jodie Poindexter? Do birds have wings?

"Sure." I turn up the walk to her house and sit awkwardly down on the step near the top. The same step where Jodie's sitting about four feet away from me. She smells like fresh apples, probably because she's eating one. *Was* eating one. She throws the core into the shrubbery and wipes a hand on her jeans.

What do I say next? I wonder. *I saw you sitting on your roof in your underwear once?*

"Yeah," Jodie says. "Sara's sister said you got in trouble with the vice principal because you wouldn't tell him what the initials on your T-shirt meant."

I'm glad I've got my jacket on and she can't see my shirt. "It's all pretty dumb," I say.

"So what does 'CM' mean? Something obscene?" She grins.

"No, something obscure," I tell her, hoping I sound like a high school senior. "Funkhouser just didn't get it."

Her eyes are laughing. "So you're not going to tell me, either?"

My pulse speeds up a little. "No," I say, and repeat the line I used with Davy. "If I told you, I'd have to kill you."

She laughs then. "I saw you on your roof one night."

"Yeah. I think the architect designed these houses for roof sitters," I say. "You crawl out there too sometimes, I noticed."

"Not when I know anyone's looking, though," she says.

"It's okay," I tell her. "I can't see much in the dark." That was a clever line. It can't be me. It's got to be the T-shirt.

Jodie laughs a second time, and I wonder if I only imagine it, but it sounds like a sad laugh to me. Up close, she's still pretty, but her skin isn't as good as it looks from twenty feet away. Her forehead's broken out a little, and the ends of her hair are raggedy. She's wearing baggy pants and an old sweatshirt, but she's got great eyes. Great mouth. Beautiful teeth, when she smiles. I can't get over the fact that we're sitting here talking like this, but I don't have any illusion that she's interested in me.

"So you'll be coming to high school next year?" she asks. "You just moved here last fall, didn't you?"

"Yeah."

"That must have been hard. New neighborhood. New school. How do you like it?"

"It's okay," I tell her. "I like our house. Like the roof. Love our pool."

"I remember when they built that pool," Jodie says. "The owner built it for his wife. He didn't like to swim, so she had it all to herself. No kids. Then she died. Can you imagine?"

I'm not sure what I'm supposed to imagine. Having a pool all to myself, or dying?

"It's sort of nice having a pool to yourself," I tell her. "I like to swim in the early morning. Next summer—well, you're welcome to come over and swim any time." She doesn't say anything, so I just keep going. "I mean, early morning or the middle of the night or anytime at all. You don't even have to ask first or call or anything. Just come on over." I'm running off at the mouth and can't stop. "The gate opens from the inside, so you have to reach your arm over, but nobody will ask what you're doing or anything. . . ."

"Hey, Kenny, I get it," she says. "Thanks."

I'm embarrassed then. We sit for another ten seconds or so without saying anything, and I wonder if I should just tell her I have to go, then leave. Wonder who's supposed to get up first, since she invited me to sit down.

What I really want to say is, *I like to watch you in the moonlight.* What I want to say is, *I notice the guy with the gorilla build doesn't come around anymore.* What I want to say is, *You don't have to be sad, because I know a dozen guys at least who would ask you out.*

But instead I hear myself saying, "Do you like crickets?" And I can't believe I said that.

"What?"

"Crickets."

"Bugs?" she asks. "Not especially."

There's nothing to do but keep going. "When I'd swim in the mornings," I tell her, "I'd find these crickets. They jump in the pool the night before, and—depending how long they've been in there—some are still alive, clinging to a leaf or something. And every morning before I'd swim, I'd go around rescuing crickets before they got swept into the skimmer box."

"And the point of this story is . . . ?"

"That sometimes I'd just flick them out, and they'd jump back in again. I mean, they don't even realize they're rescued. Don't even know where they are. It's sort of strange to think about, you know? I mean . . ." *Why don't I just shut up?* "Do you ever consider the possibility that we think this world is all we've got—get up, go to school, come home, eat dinner—when actually we're like . . . sitting on the hand of some cosmic giant bigger than our sun, and at any moment he could flick us off and annihilate the human race? Or maybe he's already saved us from some cosmic cataclysm we didn't know about. We go on reading the newspaper about little battles here on Earth, when all this turmoil's going on in space and time. We keep getting in the same mess over and over again, clinging to a leaf, our lifeboat, and we don't even realize the leaf is *nothing!*"

She's *really* staring at me now. "Wow!"

Man, I don't know what's wrong with me. It's like I have the runs, but at the wrong end of my body. "Guess I got carried away," I say miserably, staring at our house across the street and wishing I was there.

But Jodie says, "You know, you're the first person I ever knew who thinks about things like that, Kenny! I mean, what if we *are* just the playthings of somebody so huge we can't even see him, and *he's* the plaything of somebody *he* can't see, who's the plaything of somebody else. . . . What if we're completely oblivious to what's *really* about to happen to us, and all the things we're worried about now really don't matter. I've had *that* thought before. . . ."

The phone is ringing inside the house. I can hear it faintly and hope she can't, but she does.

"To be continued," she says with a laugh, and gets up. "I'll see you around."

twelve

I'm thinking maybe I was wrong about Jodie. She seems pretty normal. Everyone has a right to be sad now and then. But I think I've got a pretty good sense of how somebody feels even when I'm *not* wearing my Cricket Man T-shirt. So I'm going to keep an eye on her anyway, even though the roof sitting is probably over till next spring.

It rains almost every day, and it's cold. "The rainiest November on record," the Weather Channel says, which means skating's out too. We sure aren't getting very far with our grinds and broadslides.

I get antsy if I sit around too long, though. I miss our pool, so Luis and I start going to the county swim center on weekends. James doesn't like to swim, so Luis and I hop a bus and ride the three miles to the center.

The Calderons are definitely more upscale than James's

family or mine, but they seem to like his hanging around with James and me—glad he has a friend, I guess. Mr. Calderon is so convinced we're a good influence on Luis that he wrote to Tony Hawk once and got three autographs as a birthday present for Luis—one for Luis, one for me, and one for James.

He didn't have to do that. Luis is younger, but he's a good guy—always up, always willing to try a new trick, lets insults roll off when they happen. We look out for him.

Luis and I go to the pool to mess around, mainly. Once in a while, if the line's not too long, we climb to the top of the waterslide that stretches from one end of the long pool to the other and make like a luge as we go down, arms glued to our sides, legs straight out. But the slide's for younger kids mostly; I like to watch the divers in the deep end.

Each time, we walk past a poster out in the pool area promoting the dive team: ONE PART ACROBAT, TWO PARTS TEST PILOT. I like that. I'm thinking maybe I'll try out for the diving team in high school.

The locker room at a public pool is an education. You get a glimpse of what you looked like at three. At seven. What you'll look like at forty . . . eighty. You tell yourself that no matter what, you won't let your belly sag like that, and then you realize that these old men probably vowed the same thing when they were young. Yet somebody still loves them. Even sleeps with them, maybe. Life's amazing.

Another reason I like to go to the swim center on Saturdays is to escape all the wedding talk. Marlene and Mom start out every Saturday to look at dresses. They go to caterers to sample food, florists to look at flowers, stationery stores to look at invitations, photographers to look at pictures.

It's a relief in a way to be out of the house, because there's a sort of distance between me and my folks since the whole T-shirt thing. It's the first time I've kept something from them. I mean, that they *know* I'm doing it. The fact that I'm keeping a T-shirt logo secret really upsets them, like it represents something huge and horrible.

They drop it, though. Every so often, when no one's looking, Davy gives me the thumbs-up sign to show *he* remembers what it means. And I wish I hadn't told him.

I see Jodie, just to wave.

"Hey, Kenny!" she'll call sometimes as she's going up the steps to her house. She must have her license, because she's driving a red Toyota to school now. Her guy's still out of the picture, I guess. Jodie hasn't invited me over to continue our talk about cosmic giants, so I figure she's chalked me up as some weird middle schooler. It's nice, though, that she still says hello.

The Friday after Thanksgiving, Luis and I get on the bus again to the swim center. It's packed. We figure every kid in Montgomery County has been kicked out of the house and told to go *any*where. Do *any*thing. If you're not at the mall on the first day of Christmas shopping, you're at the swim center. The lane markers have been removed from the four-foot part of the Olympic-size pool for a family free-for-all. On the deep side, the markers are still there for lap swimmers, and the eighteen-foot diving well is reserved for divers.

Already the line for the waterslide reaches halfway along one end of the pool, and a lifeguard's checking the height of the smaller kids to make sure they're tall enough to use it. We head for the diving well.

There's a lot of attitude on the diving boards, just as there is in skating. You line up for one of the boards if you want to jump or dive, and when it's your turn, you go onto the board like there aren't thirty people watching you, and you do your thing. Sometimes you just cannonball for the heck of it to see how far your splash will reach, and sometimes you dive to see if you can top the person who went before you.

Luis sticks to jumps and doesn't much care for attitude. He tries to add a somersault a time or two, but it doesn't work. I dive, but it's crude compared to the pros, and after a while, I decide to quit making a fool of myself, and Luis and I head for the four-foot section. It's pretty crowded, though, and the noise is deafening. The two lifeguards—

a red-haired guy built like a boxcar and a slim guy with a ponytail—blow their whistles regularly, but whatever they're blowing about doesn't seem to stop.

You have to be careful during the family swim. Kids jump in wherever there's an open spot, and some places where there isn't. Swim too close to the side when kids are jumping in and you'll get a foot in the face. Anyone who can't swim is supposed to be over in the two-foot pool where the waterslide ends.

Swimming indoors is not like swimming at home, and I miss that. Miss the birds, the neighborhood cats, the occasional drone of a plane off in the distance or air conditioners turning off and on. No voices, though. No people yelling. No shouts. Just the sound of my own splash in the water.

We swim for about a half hour, and then I signal Luis that I'm ready to pack it in. He swims toward me, and it's just then that I see this kid on the bottom of the pool.

He's probably about eight or nine, wearing tan trunks, and at first I think he's trying to swim between someone's legs. Then I see that he's not moving—it's like he's just floating, facedown, on the bottom.

I suck in a deep breath, push a girl aside, and go under, angling my body down . . . down . . . cupping my hands and parting the water, kicking hard to keep myself propelled until I touch the kid in the tan trunks. I grab hold of his arm and tow him clumsily to the surface, gasping as my face hits the air, bringing his head up out of the water.

"Let him through!" Luis is yelling. "Someone's drowning! Let him through!"

People turn and stare and awkwardly move out of the way, bumping into one another in the water. The slim lifeguard's whistle is going full blast as he leaps down from his perch and jumps over the side, reaching out one long, freckled arm to grab the boy and pull him to the edge of the pool.

On the other side, the second lifeguard's standing up to see what's happening, and people look in the direction he's staring. The noise level drops as more and more people look our way. The pool manager's running out of the office there at one side.

"I got him! I got him!" the lifeguard with the freckled arm yells, moving between me and the boy I pulled up from the bottom, loosening my grip.

"Kenny found him!" Luis is saying loudly as the pool manager reaches down to hoist the kid up.

"What happened?" the manager asks the guard.

"Kid was on the bottom, but I got him," the lifeguard says.

"*Kenny* got him!" Luis yells again.

But the lifeguard blocks us with his body as he hands up the boy's feet, and then I can't see what's happening. The pool manager's kneeling down—giving CPR, maybe—and a man's crawling out of the pool saying he's the neighbor who brought the boy, a friend of his son.

The next glimpse I get, the kid's on his side and he's vomiting, and then we know he's okay. I can see the pool manager rock back on his heels, relieved. The neighbor squats down beside them, arms balanced on his knees, looking stunned.

The girl I pushed aside has made her way to the edge of the pool. "This is the person who rescued him," she says to the pool manager, pointing to me. "He's the one who brought him up."

The manager gives me a quick glance.

The freckled lifeguard looks at me. "Thanks," he says, and turns away again.

Then they've got the kid sitting up, and when he's on his feet, they take him into the office. The noise in the pool starts up again. People move away. People start to swim.

The girl is glaring after the lifeguard.

"It's okay," I tell her. She shrugs and swims off with a friend.

I look around for Luis. He's glaring after the lifeguard too. "That asshole," he mutters. "He wasn't even looking our way. He didn't even see that kid."

"It's okay," I say again. "Let's go home."

X X X

When the weekly *Gazette* comes out, there's a picture of the lifeguard and the kid, minus the puke on his face. I never even got a good look at him, but here he is—small, elfish.

Eight-year-old Jon Schaffer smiles at the lifeguard who pulled him from the water last Friday, the caption reads.

That really sucks, I tell myself. I'm lying on the couch, looking up at an almost invisible cobweb spun between a window frame and the wall. I'm thinking how weird it is that at school I'm a hero for not telling Funkhouser about my T-shirt, and here I'm a nobody after saving a kid's life. And yet it's like a secret, in a way. It doesn't matter if anyone else knows about the rescue or not. *Cricket Man knows.*

thirteen

Jodie's just getting home the next time she calls to me. I'm walking back from the bus stop, and from a half block away, I see the Toyota drive up and park in front of her house. She doesn't get out right away. Listening to the radio, probably. Then she gets out, reaches for her purse and backpack, and starts up the sidewalk.

"Hey, Kenny!" she calls when she sees me, and waits till I get a little closer. "I want to show you something. Come on in."

"Sure," I say, and cross her lawn. I'm nervous, though. I don't know how to act around her. *Be natural* just doesn't cut it.

She pulls a glove off with her teeth and holds it while she fishes in her pocket for the key. From three feet away, I can see the tiny mole on her neck, the tooth that's not quite even with the others. The real-life version, not the fantasy. But I also notice that she doesn't seem to dress as carefully as she used to. The jacket looks like a baseball jacket from an ex-boyfriend. Her jeans are baggy like before and her hair's sort of stringy.

I figure no one's home when we go inside, but I hear noises in the kitchen.

"Hi, Maria," Jodie calls, and a thin little woman comes to the kitchen doorway, smiles, and disappears again. "Cook," Jodie tells me.

I look puzzled.

"Mom and Dad get home too late to cook, and Dad won't eat carryout every night. So three times a week Maria comes by and makes stuff for dinner. And sometimes I cook," Jodie says.

"Smells good," I say, and remember that her folks have an office in DC—Poindexter and Poindexter.

"Anyway," says Jodie, taking off her jacket, "I was going through some stuff last night . . . things I collected when I was little . . . and I found this." She goes over to a pile of picture books on a corner table and sorts through them, then smiles when she finds the one she wants. "Did you ever read this?"

It's a Dr. Seuss book, *Horton Hears a Who!*

"Yeah," I say, wondering.

"Remember what we were talking about the other day —

that maybe we're only specks on the back of a giant's hand?"

I find myself grinning too, and I sit down on the edge of the couch to thumb through the book. I've got one foot resting on the side of the other again, and I quickly slide it down onto the rug. When I get to the sixth page, Jodie leans over from her chair and reads two of those lines out loud:

I'll just have to save him. Because, after all,
A person's a person, no matter how small.

"I remember this," I say. "I think Marlene read it to me once. Marlene or Mom."

"I just thought it was interesting," Jodie says, "because here it's the microscopic world that knows the score and the giants who don't have a clue." And then she says, "Want some grapes?"

"I guess so," I say. This is sure a weirdly interesting day. I wouldn't have guessed in a million years that I'd be invited to the house of a junior in high school to read a Dr. Seuss book and eat grapes. Part of me wonders if she's just messing with me—inviting this weirdo over to eat grapes and read Dr. Seuss, and then laughing about it at school the next day.

Jodie kicks her shoes off and heads for the kitchen. "Maria, do we still have some of those black grapes?" I hear her saying, and she comes back with two saucers, one for each of us.

"So what got you started looking through picture books?" I ask.

"I don't know. Sometimes I hold on to things too long, I think," she says.

I take another grape and quietly spit the seeds out in my hand, wishing she had the seedless kind. Some day there won't be any fruit left on the market with seeds, but how do things regenerate if they don't have seeds? Maybe if I can't think of anything more to talk about, I could bring that up.

"*Sometimes,*" Jodie goes on, "I think, wouldn't it be great if you had a memento, a token, of each major scene in your life—good or bad—and if you ever wanted to erase that scene from your memory, all you had to do was throw away the token and you'd never think of it again? Like it never happened? Like everything connected with it just disappeared?"

I try to decide what scenes I'd erase from my memory. I can't come up with anything specific, so I ask her, "What would you like to erase?"

She's holding a grape between her lips, her mouth in an O shape, but her lips slowly stretch into a mischievous smile. "If I wanted to *forget*, would I tell *you?*"

"Guess not," I say. I eat the last three grapes slowly

because I'm not sure what I'm supposed to do when they're gone. "Well," I say finally, "I'd better go."

She shrugs as though she doesn't care one way or the other. "My parents never get home before seven. Come over sometime if you want. Maria doesn't like me jabbering to her if she's following a recipe, so it gets pretty quiet here. But if she's making something good, we can be the testers."

Man, I think she means it! I try not to smile too wide. "Okay, then. See you."

She waves one stockinged foot at me as I head for the door. "Bye."

She's looking for company, but as I cross the street, I realize that probably anyone would do. She's still sad; she must have fallen hard for that guy. The more I think about it, in fact, I might even call her depressed, but what do I know? Anything I know about girls I've learned from Marlene, and that doesn't seem to be helping much here.

At dinner Mom says, "I noticed you stopping in at the Poindexters' this afternoon, Kenny. I didn't know that you and Jodie were friends."

"Anything wrong with being friends?" I ask, and I don't smile, either. Mothers not only look out windows, they see through walls. Through cement blocks; two-inch steel, even. But they're especially good at foreheads.

"No, of course not. I just didn't realize you knew her that well."

"We talk some," I say. "She just wanted to show me a book." And I help myself to the sweet potatoes.

More clinking of forks. More chewing.

"Isn't she a senior?" asks Dad.

"Junior," I say. Then I decide to be generous and answer the question they didn't ask. "Her parents don't get home till after seven, so she's just there with the cook. She's bored, I think."

Dad focuses on "bored." "A girl like Jodie Poindexter is *bored*?" he says. "I'd think she'd be out driving around with friends."

Mom focuses on "cook." "Their family has a cook?"

I don't tell them it's only three days a week, because *both* my parents would worry about the two days Jodie would be there alone. As though there were going to be other invitations to come over. "She says her dad hates carryout," I add.

But Marlene's not interested in talking about anyone other than Marlene. Marlene's *wedding*, to be precise.

"Dad," she begins, "please don't say no until you've listened to the whole plan. . . ."

I can see Dad's face tense a little. He's trying to look pleasant, though.

"I've decided on a color scheme for the wedding," Marlene says. "Mauve and ivory."

"What's mauve?" Davy asks.

"Between rose and lavender," says Marlene. "It's very subtle. The flowers will be mauve and the ribbon ivory. The invitations, the favors, the almonds, the frosting, the brides-maids' dresses—all mauve." She pauses and leans toward him. "All I'm asking of you is that for six hours—okay, eight maybe—eight hours of the most important day of my life—*all* I'm asking is that you wear a mauve cummerbund with your tux."

"What's a cummerbund?" Davy asks.

"A big fat sash around your waist," I tell him, and he snickers. Marlene glares at me.

"Now, Marlene . . . ," Dad begins. Dad hates dressing up at all, but asking him to wear what sounds like a woman's scarf is pretty bad.

"Only eight hours, Dad!" Marlene begs. "You can even take it off at the reception if you want, but I'm the only daughter you've got, and is eight hours out of an entire life-time too much to ask?"

"The florist suggests little touches of navy blue here and there—the bows, the flower arrangement," Mom adds. "This will give the wedding a little more masculine appeal." She looks pleadingly at Dad, and finally he sighs and smiles. That means he's going to go along with it, so everyone relaxes and we enjoy Mom's apple cobbler with ice cream.

And I'm suddenly thinking about Jodie, sitting at the table across the street each evening with her attorney parents, and

I'm wondering why she *isn't* out with friends, like Dad says. Why her folks haven't noticed, or why they don't do something about it, if they have. Well, *I've* noticed, and if nobody else is going to check up on her, I will. I'll be a Neighborhood Watch of one.

Christmas seems to perk up Jodie's spirits, because the next time we speak to each other, she's going into her house carrying shopping bags.

"Christmas shopping," she calls over, grinning.

"Get anything for me?" I joke.

"No, but what do you want?" she asks.

For once I have a comeback. "A Mercedes would be nice. Jaguar, maybe."

"I'll see what I can do." She laughs.

And once again I wonder if I was wrong about her being depressed. I see her getting into her car a day later with a couple of girlfriends. They're laughing, and she doesn't even seem to know I'm around. She doesn't call and she doesn't wave.

And so our family does Christmas.

Marlene and Owen go to the midnight service with us at church. Marlene loves for them to go places as an engaged couple. And I notice she doesn't hold her hymnbook from underneath like most people do, but rests her left hand on top of the page so her diamond catches the flicker of candlelight.

We open our presents late Christmas morning after Owen drives over in his Honda. I give Davy a spy kit—goggles for night vision, a book on deciphering codes, a telescope that lets you see around corners, invisible ink—the whole nine yards. I give Owen a framed photograph from me of Marlene as a potbellied four-year-old, and that gets a lot of laughs. There are the usual sweaters and books and games and computer stuff.

But at the very back of the tree is this tiny box with my name on it.

"Who's this from?" I ask, looking around. No one seems to know. Then Davy confesses that the girl across the street brought it over and asked him to hide it beneath our tree.

"Jodie?" I say.

"Aha!" says Owen, like he knows who she is.

I pull off the red and white polka-dot wrapping paper and the red bow and open the box. Inside is a little ceramic animal, a jaguar. And a note says, *I tried to buy you the other kind, but it wouldn't fit in the box.*

Wow. I think I'm blushing a little. I just laugh and put the box aside. A joke present, that's all. At the same time I'm thinking, I'm Jodie's friend now, sort of. And friends look out for each other.

That night I dream that Jodie Poindexter is standing on

the roof of her porch and I'm on the roof of mine, looking over at her. She's holding two shopping bags, just as she was a week ago, and she's smiling at me. No, she's laughing. I can hear her laughing as she takes a step forward. Then another. She's right at the edge of her roof, and I'm screaming, but my throat doesn't make a sound. And Jodie, still smiling, walks right off the edge.

fourteen

James and Luis and I talk about getting together New Year's Eve. I tell them they can come over and we'll watch videos, order pizza—whatever they want.

But Luis's mom won't let him out of the house. She says that a twelve-year-old Latino kid out on the streets on New Year's Eve is like a lamb in a jungle, and never mind that all he has to do is walk from their car to my house. *Nobody* should be out on the streets on New Year's Eve in the United States, given the climate, she says, and she's not talking weather. What she really means, of course, is that she's not sure she can trust us to *stay* inside once she delivers Luis.

So it's only James coming over for New Year's Eve. Marlene and Owen are at a party and won't be home till morning, while Mom and Dad and Davy are having dinner with family friends. I get some foot-long hot dogs for

James and me. We end up watching crashes from the Indianapolis 500.

I think we miscount the number of dogs we eat. Or else it's the super-dense chocolate torte Mom leaves for us in the fridge. Actually, it's probably the rum we pour in our Cokes, but James throws up in the hallway, and after we clean that up, it definitely puts a damper on the evening. He decides to go home around nine thirty. We only live about six blocks apart, but he won't let me walk him home, so I stand at the door and make sure he's not weaving around when he walks. He says he'll call me when he gets home.

I barely close the door when the phone rings. It's Jodie.

"I saw your friend leave," she says. "You alone?"

"Yeah . . . ," I say, wondering.

"I'm bored, and misery loves company," she tells me. Man oh man! New Year's Eve and Jodie Poindexter's lonely.

"So why aren't you out at a party or something?" I ask. "Everyone else is."

"Everyone but you," she answers.

"Well, I tried to have a party, but only James could come. We drank rum and Cokes and James got sick. He threw up all over the rug and part of the wall."

"That's too much information, Kenny," she says, so I shut up and let her figure out what to talk about next.

"My parents are at some big attorney's house for a party. Formal. Tux and everything," Jodie goes on.

I don't know what to say, so I ask, "You want to come over here?"

"Really? It's okay if I come over?"

My hands feel clammy and my heart begins to pound. *Can this be happening?*

"Um . . . of course. There's nobody here but—" Then I hear Dad's car in the driveway. "Well, there is now."

"Oh, I don't really want to come over and sit around talking with your parents," Jodie says. "It's been . . . sort of a rough evening. I'm not in the mood to be nice."

I think about that. "Well, you could wait till they go to bed. They never stay up on New Year's Eve. Guaranteed."

"Sure?"

"Yeah. I'll call you as soon as everyone's asleep," I say. "We can sit out on the roof or something."

She gives a little laugh that I never heard before.

"All right," she says.

"I'll call you," I say again as I hear Dad's key in the lock.

Am I insane? Jodie and me on the *roof*? How do you entertain a girl on New Year's Eve? What do we *do*? What do we *talk* about? What do we *eat*?

I imagine Jodie Poindexter choking on an olive and Cricket Man giving the Heimlich maneuver. I imagine Jodie rolling off the roof and Cricket Man rescuing her just as she reaches the rain gutter. Nothing normal comes to mind.

I begin to worry that this will be the one year Mom and Dad decide to stay up late and watch the ball drop in Times Square. They've never done it yet that I know of. Marlene and I are the night owls in the family. All you have to do is yawn in Davy's direction, and his eyes will start to close.

This time, though, they've had a late dinner, and Mom always says it's not a good idea to go to bed on a full stomach. If I asked if I could go over to Jodie's instead—Jodie and me alone in her house on New Year's Eve—you can bet your life that the answer would be no.

"Where's James?" asks mom.

"He didn't feel good so he went home," I tell her. "I'm going to call and see how he's doing."

"That's too bad. And on New Year's Eve," says Dad.

Nina answers the phone.

"Oh, it's Kenny!" she says, and tries to make her voice sound sexy. "Happy New Year, Kenny!"

"Hi," I mumble. "Can I talk to James?"

"I don't know," she says, and giggles. "Something the matter with your voice? You sound all right to me."

"*May* I talk to James?" I say impatiently.

"Maybe, but you have to talk to me first," she says. "You got big plans for tonight?" Then I hear James shouting at her in the background, and finally he's on the line. He says he's okay, but he threw up again in their front yard.

"Happy New Year," I tell him.

By ten thirty Davy has gone to bed, and Mom and Dad soon follow. At five after eleven, I'm standing outside their bedroom door, listening to Dad's snoring, and then I go to the phone and call Jodie.

"All clear," I say, like a spy or something. "Don't ring the doorbell."

"I won't."

I get some crackers from the kitchen, open a can of black olives, and grab a handful of candy bars from a bag that's been sitting around since Halloween. I go to the window by the porch and watch for Jodie's silhouette against the streetlights, but I don't see her. Something taps the glass beside my face and I jump. She's right outside the window, and I can see her smiling at me in the dark.

I quietly open the door, and we're both laughing silently. She's holding one hand over her mouth.

"Are they in bed?" she whispers.

"Yeah. Come on up. But stick to the wall. Some of the stairs squeak in the middle," I tell her. Then, "You going to be warm enough?"

"I hope so," she says. She's only got on a fleece jacket. I grab an old wool jacket from the hall closet to take upstairs with us.

Jodie looks around, trying to see how our house is different from theirs, I suppose. They're exactly the same model, only mirror images of each other. Then she follows me up the stairs and gives a little giggle as the third step creaks.

"Shh," I say, turning around, and again she claps one hand over her mouth. She's got her long hair in a braid down her back. It looks as though it hasn't been combed all day, but on Jodie it looks really good. Actually, on Jodie Poindexter almost everything looks good.

I haven't even thought of what I'm going to say if Mom gets up and sees me taking a girl into my bedroom. Never mind explaining the Cricket Man logo to her. How would I explain that I invited a high school junior over to crawl out my bedroom window and sit on the roof?

We stop every few steps and listen, but all is quiet, and it's a huge relief when we get into my room and close the door behind us.

"This is wild!" Jodie whispers, giggling again. "Who's in the room next to you?"

"That's Marlene's, and she's out," I say.

I've already removed the screen on my window. On the floor beside it, I've got a couple of glasses, an opened bottle of Sprite, the rest of the rum, and the food I collected downstairs.

"Wait a minute," I say as she starts toward the window. I pull the blanket off my bed and grab both my pillows. I stuff them and the wool jacket out the window first, followed by the food and drink. I crawl through the window and help Jodie out, then close the window, all but a crack.

She helps me fold the blanket so we'll have something soft to sit on, and we prop my pillows behind our backs.

I pull the wool jacket over our laps, but our legs aren't touching. I wouldn't want her to think I was getting ideas.

"So this is what it looks like from across the street," Jodie says, studying her own house.

And Cricket Man answers, "Yeah, except sometimes, if I'm lucky, there's a girl on the roof over there in her underwear." She punches me on the arm, but when I punch her back, she looks surprised and says, "Ow!" I make a mental note that when a girl punches your arm, don't punch back. I hand her one of the Mars bars and she starts eating.

"What if your folks call home and you're not there? Or come home early and find you gone?" I ask.

"They won't. I told them I'd be going to a party at Sara's and I'd spend the night there," she says.

I think this over. "And if they call Sara's?"

"She'll cover for me. I told her there was this guy I wanted to see." Jodie gives me a look. "Not you. Not anybody."

I just have to ask the question: "So how come you *aren't* at the party?"

"Because there isn't any. At least, not at Sara's. That I know of."

"And . . . you didn't want to go anywhere else?"

"Oh, everyone's dressing up. You know . . . New Year's Eve. Dancing. The works," she says.

"And you don't like to dance?"

"God! You sound like my mother!" Jodie says, and now she's mad again, so I raise my voice to a high falsetto.

"No, I don't," I squeak.

She laughs then. "Yes, you do. 'Why don't you do this? Why don't you do that?' I'm still trying to get over Gary, and she thinks it should be easy."

It's the first time she's mentioned that guy. First time I learn his name. Somehow I thought it would be Hugo or Sampson or something.

"I guess it's not easy," I say.

She leans her head against the house. "You've got that right."

I don't know what surprises me most—that she mentions Gary's name, that she tells me getting over him isn't easy, or that Jodie Poindexter doesn't even *want* to go to a party on New Year's Eve. It's like somebody else is sitting here on the roof beside me.

I reach for the box of crackers. "Want a Triscuit?" I say.

Now we're digging our hands into the box of crackers and watching the lights of a plane move slowly across the dark sky from Reagan National. It's easier to talk with a mouthful of Triscuits. Nothing you say sounds so serious when there's all that crunching going on.

"So . . . ," I say after a while. "You don't want to talk about Gary?"

Jodie's hands drop to her lap. "No, I don't. Listen. Do you have any peanut butter? These are kind of dry."

"I'll get some," I say.

"Be careful." She giggles. "And bring a knife."

I crawl to the window, raise it slowly so it won't squeak, crawl inside, and go quickly downstairs. I find a jar of extra crunchy, pick up a butter knife. Then, to make it a little special, I bring along a jar of raspberry jam to go on top of the peanut butter.

Crawling back through the window, I scoot in beside her again and hand her the peanut butter and the jam. "Remember, we've got olives, too," I say.

"Yeah. *Black* olives. Classy," says Jodie.

We use our fingers to fish for olives from the can and pull them out, dripping the dark liquid. We pop the olives into our mouths, then take a bite of Triscuit. It's not exactly easy to do in the dark, with a wool jacket for your table. One minute the jar of raspberry jam is sitting on the roof between us, and the next, it's rolling slowly down the shingles.

"Omigod!" cries Jodie. There's one second of silence, and then a *ka-PLIST!!* as it explodes on the sidewalk below.

fifteen

We can't stop laughing. Muffled, of course. We bury our faces in the wool jacket, and just when we think it's safe to sit up again, another wave of laughter sweeps over us.

"D-do you think anyone heard?" she gulps at last.

"Only the fire department over on Democracy Boulevard," I say, and that sets her off again.

But no light comes on behind us. There are no footsteps inside, no sound of a door opening.

"How are you going to explain *that* to your folks?" Jodie asks, and she can barely get the words out because she's doubled over again.

We stop laughing finally and concentrate on the olives till they're gone. I tip the can on the roof in front of us so the liquid runs out. We brush the cracker crumbs off the wool jacket and set the empty olive can up against the house so it can't roll off.

We're quiet for a while. So quiet that I glance over once to see if she's asleep. She's not—just staring out at the streetlights, thinking of Gary, probably.

So I say, "I can't understand why it wouldn't help you get over him to go out more with your friends."

"Because it wouldn't be the same," says Jodie.

"It's still better than sitting home alone feeling sorry for yourself," I tell her, and I can almost feel her body stiffen, even though we're not touching.

"Who says I'm feeling sorry for myself?" she snaps. "Is that why you asked me over?"

"No! Look! I'm sorry!" I say. "I just . . . well . . . sort of worry about you sometimes."

That doesn't help. She's looking daggers at me. "What do you really know about me?"

I'm getting in over my head and I know it. Cricket Man comes to the rescue. "Uh . . . Jodie Poindexter, only daughter of two Washington lawyers, age sixteen, drives a red Toyota . . . That's about it, I guess."

"All right, let me ask you. Why aren't *you* out at a party?" she wants to know.

"I'm not Mr. Popularity," I say. "Never have been."

She sighs. "So here we are, on a cold and beautiful

New Year's Eve, sitting on a porch roof eating Triscuits. *Dry* Triscuits," she says. "Damn that jelly."

"And olives. We had olives. Don't forget those." I've got her smiling again. There's just enough light from the streetlamps to see her lips stretching at the corners.

Just then we hear firecrackers going off somewhere in the neighborhood.

"Is it midnight?" she asks. She can't see her watch. A couple of horns start blowing.

"Must be," I say. I pour the rest of the Sprite into our glasses. "Want some rum?" She nods, and I pour a little of that in too. I kind of clink my glass against hers. "So," I say. "Happy New Year. Or maybe, *Happier* New Year?"

Jodie takes a sip of Sprite. And then she starts to cry.

I don't know what to say, because I don't know what's going on. She didn't expect me to *kiss* her, did she?

"What's wrong?" I ask, but she puts her head down between her knees.

"Oh God," she weeps, and sounds angry and disgusted both. *"Look* at me! What the heck am I doing over here on New Year's Eve?"

It's like her words have stingers on them. I thought she was having a good time. It's not as though I didn't try. . . .

"If you'll tell me what's wrong . . . ," I say.

"Oh *God!*" she says again, and cries some more.

"*Every*thing's wrong. My whole crappy life is wrong, that's what's wrong."

Finally she stops sobbing and leans back again, eyes closed, like she's exhausted. I'm afraid to say a word. To move, even. I'm glad she quiets down, because I don't want my parents to hear.

It seems like an hour goes by. Probably only two or three minutes. But finally Jodie says, "I'm sorry."

I don't answer. Partly because I'm pissed, and partly because I'm afraid it'll make things worse. I don't know how I feel about Jodie any longer. Sorry for her? Angry at her? I think . . . maybe worried about her more than anything else.

"When you're little," Jodie goes on, her voice tired-sounding, "it's like . . . like you'll know what to do when you're older. Like whatever you want, you'll figure out how to get. You'll know what to do." She sniffles. "You think growing up means you can solve anything. But you can't."

"Some things work out," I say. Mr. Positive here.

"Hardly *anything*!" Jodie says. "Problems start coming at you, and sometimes when you think you've solved one, it only makes things worse."

I don't answer, and Jodie goes on: "*Think* about it— all the misunderstandings that can happen between two people. *Two people!* And if two people can't get along, how can you expect two religions to get along? Two races? Two *countries*? It's impossible! We're never going to solve anything. People will just go on having kids they don't want and getting divorced and polluting the earth and going to war. . . ."

If Jodie Poindexter wasn't depressed, I sure was. What kind of New Year's Eve is it if you're going to sit on a roof talking about war? But she's unstoppable.

"Do you know what really pulled this country out of the Great Depression, Kenny? We talked about it in history. You know about the Great Depression, don't you?"

"Franklin Delano Roosevelt?" I say, and I only know that because he was president.

"Yes. Men were out of work and they were hungry and there were breadlines, and some people say Roosevelt pulled us through because he started public projects that put men back to work. But you know what *really* pulled us through?" she goes on.

She's already asked that once. "I bet you're going to tell me," I say.

"War," says Jodie. "When World War II happened. Suddenly this country needed tanks and guns to fight Hitler. Factories geared up, men went back to work, people had more money, they started spending, and . . . *Bam!* America's great again. Isn't that *depressing*?"

I'm confused. "You a history major? How did we get to World War II?"

"Because it took a war to solve the problem!" she says vehemently. "It took guns and bombs and killing people to get us back on our feet. And who do you suppose is profiting from what's going on in Iraq?"

This can't *be why Jodie was crying*, I tell myself, but I try to think like a high school junior—*this* high school junior, anyway—and it's sort of beginning to make sense.

"Well," I tell her, my mind racing on ahead of me, "then I've got a solution."

Jodie glances over at me and pulls the wool jacket up under her chin. "Yeah, right," she mutters.

"Really!" I say, wondering why nobody ever thought of it before. "All these factories making stuff that's totally useless except to kill people, right? And yet it helps the economy?"

"So?"

"So here's my solution: Get a lot of factories making . . . um . . . square wheels."

"*What?*"

"Can you think of anything more useless? But at least square wheels won't hurt anybody. Factories speed up production, more men go back to work, and instead of a lot of old tanks rusting out on battlefields when a war's over, the government will have piles of square wheels to bury in a mountain somewhere."

Jodie stares at me, then starts to laugh.

"Shh," I say, afraid she'll wake my parents.

She shakes her head. "All this time I've been living across the street from a certified lunatic."

"Anything to make you laugh," I say. Then I take a chance and add, "I never know what's going to set you off."

I can't decide if she's amused or annoyed. "God, Kenny, am I that pathetic? I don't want you on my case too."

"Who else is on your case?" I ask.

"Gary. My parents. My teachers. I'm one big disappointment. But I really, really didn't come over to cry on your shoulder."

I rub my shoulder. "Feels dry to me."

No smile from Jodie. "I just get . . . these moods sometimes. But I had fun tonight. Really. Thanks for the crackers and olives. I'd better get home, I think."

She hands me the wool jacket and crawls toward the window. Silently she lifts the pane and crawls back through. I pass her the glasses and the olive can, the Sprite bottle and the blanket. Then we silently slip back downstairs, testing for squeaky floorboards, and I open the front door.

"Watch for the raspberry jam," I say, and she gives this little snort.

"I will," she says in a tiny voice, and I don't have to see her face to know that she's smiling and crying at the same time.

I think about the stuff she was saying, about kids with parents who don't want them, parents who are getting divorced, people going off to war, and I wonder just what's happening at her place.

I watch her cross the street, watch her open her front door and go inside. I don't know what's the matter with Jodie, but I'm going to find out.

sixteen

De•pres•sion\di'pre-shən\n(14c): a psychoneurotic disorder marked by sadness, inactivity, difficulty in thinking and concentration, and feelings of dejection and hopelessness, and sometimes suicidal tendencies. . . .

If Webster's is right, Jodie Poindexter is depressed. I close the dictionary and turn on my computer. I type in "How can I help a depressed person?" and Google comes up with "best things to say":

> *I love you.* No way.
>
> *I care.* Maybe.
>
> *I'm not going to abandon you.* Doubtful.
>
> *Do you need a hug?* Yeah, right.
>
> *If you need a friend, I'm here.* Maybe I can use that one too.

When all this is over, I'll still be here and so will you. How can I possibly say that when I have no idea what Jodie might do next? If she *is* depressed, that is, and not just bored with me and mad that I was the best she could do on New Year's Eve.

I decide to check in with her every so often. Call her now and then. And if I get really worried about her—I mean, *really* worried—I'll tell someone. Her parents, maybe. My parents, anyway.

Half of January goes by, though, and I don't hear from Jodie. And I chicken out—I only call her once, when I knew no one was home. I figure she's got caller ID, so she'll know it was me, and then if she wants to talk, she'll call back. She doesn't.

I see her going in and out of her house, but she doesn't look around for me. I guess I was just her POLR (Person of Last Resort) on New Year's Eve, and the fact that she was sitting on the porch roof with me was all she needed to be able to tell her friends she "went out." Now that the second semester's begun, she's probably made a new start, has new assignments, and won't need any help from me. As though I had any to give.

There are usually a few days in January—in Maryland, anyway—that we call the "January thaw." The thin layer of snow melts fast in the bright sunshine, and even pools of water dry up on the sidewalks. The county's renovated an old skateboard park in Rockville, and they open it for a week as a test run. James used to skate there, and now he wants to see if it's improved any.

"Better than a parking garage, man," he tells me on Wednesday. "We could pick up our boards after school and head for Rockville."

We run it by Luis. He says he'll come, except that his mom's nervous about Rockville, so he's not going to say where we're going.

"What's wrong with Rockville?" I ask.

He shrugs. "Just another place they don't know much about. After what happened in Silver Spring . . ."

"You mean the parking garage?" I ask. "Did Farthouse call your parents too?"

"No, but if he ever did, I couldn't hang out with you guys for the rest of my life," says Luis. "The one big thing they don't want for our family is trouble."

James gives him a look. "'Cause you're Hispanic?"

"Man, some day you'll be the majority," I say.

"Yeah," says Luis. "That's what everyone's afraid of."

At my place, we ask Mom for a ride to Rockville, tell her we'll take a bus back.

There are a bunch of other guys skating. We're all idiots, because it hurts worse when you get banged up on cold concrete. But if we could skate like some of these guys, we'd probably be showing off every day of the year.

Two of them, two of the best, sort of take turns being the audience for each other. Except they don't clap or cheer or anything. Don't say anything at all, actually. Just wait till the trick's over and then the other guy is on. Everyone else makes room.

At first it's nothing special—a frontside noseslide—and after that a 50-50, bringing the axles of both trucks straddling the railing. Then the second guy takes over, does a 360 shove-it, the board spinning around under his feet. But these guys take turns doing wallrides. They're like Spider-Man there on the vert, and each one comes down easy, body in a crouch, and gets upright again.

"Oh, man!" says Luis. "Wish I could do that!"

It's an okay skate park, nothing great. A mix of concrete and wood. Lots of ramps and banks and rails, including a six-stair rail with the wall at one end. James says they've added some street stuff—pyramids, planter boxes, a park bench to ride on and over.

We've been there only twenty minutes or so when Luis asks what time it is. I glance at my watch. "Four thirty-five," I tell him. And then I try this new trick—the pop shove-it, where you slam the tail of the board down, and when the board gets air, you shove it with your front foot so it does a 180-degree turn while you stay in the same place.

Except I don't stay in the same place. I don't even stay upright. My feet get tangled up with the board and I go skidding along the concrete, the cuff of my jacket sliding up my arm so that it feels like the flesh from my wrist to my elbow is going through an electric sander. My eyes are smarting, my arm's bleeding, and a thin flap of dirty skin hangs by a thread.

I blink a couple of times. I feel my teeth clench, yet my lips stretch mechanically into a kind of smile that everyone knows is fake. I bend to pick up my stupid board.

"You okay?" asks Luis.

"Sure," I say, and pretend I'm fine though I bruised up a leg too.

It's about five minutes later that one of the two semipro guys takes a fall that reminds you why you're supposed to wear a helmet. The Spider-Man guy is up on the wall again, but when he reverses at the top, something goes wrong, he spins through the air and his board whacks him on the head. Really whacks him.

It's bad to say, but there's something funny about it. I mean, it takes a lot of willpower not to laugh out loud. All of us are standing there trying to keep a straight face. But when this guy gets to his feet, he imitates himself, wobbling his legs, crossing his eyes, and looking goofy. So we all crack up, and he laughs with us. And I'm thinking, *Why couldn't I have done that?*

"What time is it?" Luis asks, and I want to leave too.

But James is annoyed. "Who cares?" he barks to Luis. "Why didn't you bring a watch if you're so worried?"

Luis shrugs. "Lost it, I guess."

James dismisses him with a look. We never want to stay as long as he does. But finally he packs it in, and we leave for the bus stop—Luis worrying about the time, James muttering in disgust, me with an arm that feels on fire.

Maybe Cricket Man's services aren't needed as much as I'd thought. I get a wave now and then from Jodie, but we don't call each other. She gets into her Toyota each morning and goes to school. Has her backpack with her, anyway. Once in a while she'll drive off with a couple of girls. There was even a guy over there once, but I think he was with one of the friends.

Around Valentine's Day, the high school has one of its two formal dances of the year, the Snow Ball. Last year I looked out my window to see a limo coming to pick Jodie up. It was huge—like it stretched all the way down the block, a row of lights along the sides.

I watched Jodie and her date—the guy who preceded Gary—come down the porch steps, Jodie in a slinky red dress that could have set the fire department on fire—that and the slit up the side, which I noticed when she reached the bottom step. She had a short, furry thing around her shoulders, and the limo driver opened the door for her as she climbed in.

I figure that Jodie will go to the Snow Ball again this year with somebody new, and that'll be the end of missing Gary. The *Gazette* lists the date of the Snow Ball as Friday, February 13, so I keep my eyes on the street below, watching for the limo with lights.

But none comes. Of course, she could be going to the dance in somebody's Lexus—somebody's *Dad's* Lexus, even. But no car stops at the Poindexters'. Once I see Jodie pass by her living-room window, so I know she's home.

I wonder if I should call. I even put my hand on the phone once. But she'd know why I called. *Nobody asked you, huh?* my phone call would tell her. *Still not over Gary? Can't get up the nerve to ask a guy yourself?* What did that guy have that other guys don't, anyway?

For a brief moment I imagine putting on my suit, the one I wore for my grandmother's funeral—if it still fits—then going across the street and telling Jodie to get dressed, that I'll be her date for the evening. Cricket Man to the rescue.

Right. In *her* Toyota. With Jodie driving. With thirty bucks, max, in my pocket for dinner somewhere before. Oh yeah, one more thing: I can't dance.

seventeen

If Jodie comes out of her house all weekend, I don't see her. I start worrying again.

On Tuesday, though, I get home from school and there's a note from Mom saying she's taken Davy to the mall to buy pants. I stand at the kitchen counter toasting two halves of a bagel. The toaster pops and I spread one of the halves with cream cheese. I eat it, still standing, thoughts turning over and over in my head like clothes in a dryer.

Suddenly I put the other bagel half on a bread board, trim a thin slice off the top, the sides, and the bottom. Then I walk across the street to Jodie's house, and when she opens the door, I hand her the bagel half.

"For you," I say. "Square wheel."

Jodie stares at it like I'd handed her a . . . well, a bagel with the edges trimmed off. She starts to laugh. "You're crazy," she says.

She's standing there in what looks like her dad's bathrobe, and there's a tiny piece of something stuck to her upper lip. Toothpaste, maybe? It's funny how your eye will focus on some small thing like that.

"Wanna come in?" she asks, and I step inside. "So," she says, closing the door behind me. "What am I supposed to do with this?"

"Eat it?" I say, and grin. But I'm still staring at the toothpaste or cream cheese or whatever, and I'm running my tongue over my lip. As soon as I realize what I'm doing, I can't help myself; I do it again.

"What's the matter?" Jodie asks, and immediately wipes her lips, looking embarrassed. I'm an idiot, and I feel the heat creeping up my neck. I step into the living room.

"You're not sick, are you?" I ask.

Jodie gives me a quick look. "Why?"

I nod toward the bathrobe.

"I'm *cold*," she says, and I should have been able to figure that out. "Dad keeps the house at sixty-eight degrees while we're gone during the day, and I have to turn up the heat when I get home. You want a soda or anything?"

"Whatever you've got," I say lamely. Cricket Man losing his power or something? I follow her out to the kitchen. "So . . . what's been going on with you?"

"School, what else?" she says. I stand in the doorway while she gets down a couple of glasses, fills them from the ice dispenser, then opens a couple cans of Coke. The kitchen is all stainless steel with granite countertops, clean as a hospital room, which means the cook isn't working today. "Big test in Algebra Two coming up," she adds.

"I thought that was sophomore year," I say.

"Not for me, it's not. Algebra One in ninth; geometry in tenth; Algebra Two in eleventh, and solid geometry in twelfth. If I make it that far," says Jodie.

"Why wouldn't you?" I ask.

"It's hard for me," Jodie says. "I'm just barely getting through, and only because Sara comes over once or twice a week to help me with homework." She grabs a bag of chips off the counter and we go back to the living room.

The house *is* cold. She sits down on the couch in the long robe and piles sofa pillows on her lap as insulation, then rests her arms on top. If I was in love with Jodie Poindexter, I'd go over and put my arm around her, but I'm not.

I'm wondering how to ask her why she didn't go to the dance. *If* I should ask her, and I know the answer to that already. So I say, "Well, what did you do all weekend besides study?" Never mind that we hadn't said hi for the last six weeks.

"Homework, what else? Term paper coming up for history," she says, but I notice she doesn't look at me when she says it. Like she knows I know she didn't go to the Snow Ball the other night. "If you've read anything about the bubonic plague, now's the time to tell me."

"The Black Plague? Who would assign a paper on that?" I ask. I set my glass down on the polished wood coffee table and Jodie immediately picks it up, slides a magazine underneath it, and puts my glass back down again. I start to put one foot on the other, then stop myself in time.

"It wasn't assigned exactly," Jodie says. "We have to write a paper about some big event that happened in the Middle Ages, and I chose the plague." Her eyes fix on me for just a second, then she drops them again. "It's just something that always interested me . . . the fact that all these people were dying of it, and nobody knew what was causing it. They didn't know whether to leave the city for the country or wear onions around their necks or what. I always wondered what I would have done if I'd been living then."

"I read a comic book about it once," I say. Oh, boy. Every time I open my mouth, I say something even stupider than I'd said before.

"A *comic* book?"

"Yeah. It was pretty good, based on history. One of those educational comics. The thing I remember was an invading horde that was waging war on this trading post somewhere, but the men got sick with bubonic plague. When the leader saw that they were going to die of it, he

ordered that the plague-infested corpses should be cata-
pulted into the town."

Jodie's staring at me. "They made that part up."

"I don't think so. It was supposed to be based on
research."

"Yeah, right. Have a chip," she says, and hands me the
bag across the coffee table.

"Well, it's true. It was in the Crimea. Look it up," I say.

"Whatever," she says.

We're quiet for a while. I keep picking up my glass, taking a swallow, and setting it down again. On the magazine.
Then I take too big a swallow and cough.

Jodie isn't paying attention to me. "Think about it," she
says. "If suddenly people started dying in this neighborhood and we didn't know why, we wouldn't know if it was
in the air or the water or some chemical leaching through
the soil. . . ."

I finally stop coughing. "Hey, if you ever decide to write
a *fun* paper, let me know," I say, and immediately wish I
hadn't. I don't want to sound critical.

I think maybe Jodie feels comfortable talking with me,
though, because she tips back her head and sits still for a
minute. Then she says, "Mom wants me to see a psychologist."

I try not to look surprised. "Why? Because you're writ-
ing about the Black Plague?"

This makes her smile for a nanosecond, but then it disappears. "Because I stay in too much," she says. "My parents worry about everything. Whether their law firm's making enough money, whether global warming will kill us off . . ." She gives this little laugh. "Mom *used* to complain when I went out all the time. And she probably wouldn't be complaining now if my grades weren't so bad. . . ."

I'll admit my cricket sense was tingling. If ever Jodie was giving me an opening, this was it. "So why *don't* you go out more? And why *are* your grades so bad?" I ask.

She lifts her glass and takes a sip of Coke. Then another. "It's just a hard year for me, that's all," she says. And then, like the flip of a switch, she's telling me about this science teacher who picks his nose and how terrible the food is in the school cafeteria and how she's taking PE online this semester.

"What?" I say. "Seriously?"

"Yep. You can take one semester online as long as you have a biweekly conference with the PE instructor and keep an exercise log. One of your parents has to sign off on it, but that's it."

"So what do you *do*?" I ask. "Throw a ball at your screen saver?"

She laughs really hard now. I like making Jodie Poindexter laugh. "Exercise. Keep a food diary. Healthful lifestyle, that kind of thing."

I grin. "You can do anything you want on a computer."

"Everything but be happy," says Jodie. And then she tells me she has to study, so I leave.

Weather's awful for the rest of the week. All the snow that didn't fall in January comes now. It's not lightweight snow you can brush away, either. It's like vanilla pudding. Most of the time it doesn't stick around for more than a few days. Then it lazes about in big gray piles on street corners, puddles forming in the streets, and each car that goes by makes a slick, slushing sound. But this time the temperature's freezing, and there's ice where you least expect it.

James complains constantly because we can't skate outdoors, so Luis and I go over to his place to practice. He's got a homemade ramp in his garage—his dad turns the garage over to him in the winter—and James spends a lot of time in there. But we have to leave the garage door open so we don't crash into it when we come down the ramp.

As soon as his sister hears voices in the garage, she comes out to watch. No matter where I go, Nina's green eyes are on me.

"Nice one, Kenny," she'll say, when I do a kickflip.

She doesn't get it that skaters don't talk much. James tells her to go inside, she's bothering us, but she won't. It's cold in the garage too. Bone-chilling cold, but Nina sticks it out. Finally I fake a sore throat and go home.

Sometimes, though, I think it would be easier to skate in a cold garage with Nina watching than sit through a meal now with Marlene. That night I slide into my chair, late as usual, and the air is thick with wedding talk. As usual.

"Stephanie gained four pounds and they had to sew gussets in her gown," Marlene says.

Do I want to hear about gussets? Do I even know what a gusset is?

"We have to watch these calories from now until April," says Mom, taking the grated cheese from Marlene and passing it on to me.

"I'm not going to sleep until I see that dye job on the shoes," Marlene continues. "Gretchen said *her* bridesmaids' shoes came out two different shades of aqua. The same pair! The left shoe was darker than the right! A nightmare." She scrapes the butter off her roll with her fingernail and takes a bite.

"We also need to get to the caterer's, Marlene, and taste their smoked salmon. If we substitute that for the lobster risotto, we can save enough to have two more hors d'oeuvres," Mom says.

"I'm getting a tattoo on my forehead," I murmur.

Dad looks up.

"I don't know, *everyone* has smoked salmon," Marlene goes on. "And I'm definitely not giving up the crème brûlée."

"From one end of my forehead to the other," I say.

Davy's giggling now and Dad gets the joke.

"But if we have shrimp artichoke too . . . ," says Mom.

"A tattoo of what?" Dad asks, grinning.

"A naked girl. She'd have to be lying down, of course."

"What about meatballs?" says Mom. "Or an assortment of blini?"

"On his forehead?" asks Dad.

They suddenly stop talking and stare at Dad. Davy and I burst out laughing. Marlene and Mom don't have a clue.

eighteen

When I go to James's house again for practice, the garage door's closed and I can't hear anyone behind it. Luis is supposed to be here too, so I go up the steps and ring the bell. Nina answers.

She's barefoot and wearing flannel pajamas. Her toenails are painted pink and green. I feel embarrassed because I'm seeing Nina in her pajamas, and then I realize it's only the bottom part of her outfit that's pajamas, and I'm embarrassed because I'm embarrassed.

"Where's James?" I murmur. No "Hi" or "How ya doin'?" Jeez, sometimes I'm sick of myself.

Her eyes take me in and they sort of dance. I think she's smiling, but I'm not sure.

"Who shall I say is calling?" Nina asks, putting on a British accent.

Is she going to tell me or not? I wonder. "Prince Charles," I answer.

She laughs. "Come on in," she says. "James and Luis are watching a DVD down in the family room."

"Thanks," I say. She follows me over to the stairs, and as I start down, she yells to the guys, "Prince Charles and his skateboard!"

I sink down on the couch beside Luis, and James stops the disc. Goes back a little. "Watch this," he says.

It's an old skateboard DVD of pros and their friends, and there's some guy they call "The Donger," skating through San Diego.

"Look at that!" says James in awe, as the Donger ollies a chest-high bar, then skates on past two security guards and pops another ollie over an eight-stair railing.

"Now watch *this*," says Luis, and there's Tosh Townend, airborne, his blond hair in dreadlocks, bringing his skateboard down to land on a steep railing. You think it's impossible what he's doing, but he's doing it.

After an hour of this, we go out into the garage, but we should have done our practice before we watched the pros, because we suck compared to them. Still, we make some progress, and my board stays with me like there's magnets on the soles of my shoes.

"Hey, can I borrow your cell?" Luis asks me. "I need to call my mom before she calls me."

"I left it home. Battery's recharging. Where's yours?"

"I don't know," says Luis.

James shakes his head and rolls his eyes at me. I guess when a guy's family has as much money as the Calderons, you don't have to keep track of your stuff. They'll just buy you more.

Later, when we pick up our jackets to leave, Nina comes to the door. "Bye, Prince Charming," she says.

I'm the Great Stone Face. Don't even turn around as I head down the steps.

I'm doing okay at school. My popularity almost doubled because of the T-shirt thing, meaning that more kids say hi to me now in the halls. It's not like I'm getting invited to a bunch of parties or anything, or that girls are clawing at my jeans as I go up the stairs. Just respect, I guess. Weird.

Funkhouser is cold to me when we pass in the hall, but I keep out of his office and he keeps out of my business. He's less crazy than he was at the start of school, and to his credit, he's organized so much extracurricular stuff that any student who's interested has a lot to choose from.

He sets up an eight-week camera workshop in March, and I decide to sign up. If I'm serious about a career as a photographer, I'll need all the practice I can get. What I don't figure on is that Nina Lambert signs up too.

"Hey, Kenny!" she coos when I walk into room 217 after school.

I pretend I don't hear her. Don't even see her, though she's hard to miss in black tights and a purple top with beads sewn in the fabric. A purple hair thing holds up her long ponytail. I sit as far away from her as possible, while Miss Harley tells us about her years in the Peace Corps as a photographer, and how in the next three months we're going to do action shots, portraiture, and photojournalism.

I know right away that my first action shot will be James or Luis on a skateboard, suspended in the air. Portraiture? Jodie, maybe, in that old bathrobe, hugging her knees. Photojournalism—if I'm lucky, maybe something big will happen at Marlene's wedding, and Cricket Man will just happen to have his camera ready.

"Hey, Prince Charles," Nina says to me as we're leaving. "Want to do an action shot with *me*?"

If I was in the pool, and Nina was a cricket, I think I'd let her go straight into the old skimmer box.

"Yeah, right," I say, and keep walking.

Why is it so easy to talk to a really pretty girl like Jodie Poindexter, three years older than I am, and all I can do is grunt at Nina, who's only a year younger than me? All I know is that a couple days later, when I see Jodie hunched on her front steps, leafing through the mail, I ask if she wants to go for a walk.

"In the cold? Where to?"

"Anywhere. Mailbox and back. Deli and back. Mall and back. Your pick."

"I'm good for about a mile, round trip, no more than that," she says unenergetically, and zips the collar of her jacket up around her ears.

"Then let's walk over to the park by the tennis courts. Let me ditch this backpack and we'll go."

I cross the street, drop my backpack inside the front door, and call to Mom that Jodie and I are going for a walk. Then I head off with Jodie.

She doesn't look too good. I can't tell if she's sick or she's just not taking care of herself. Her hair's stringy, face is a little puffy. I'm remembering the article I read on Google about depression and mentally go through the list: loss of interest, inactivity, irritability. How can I bring it up? How can I help?

We set out at an easy pace. The collar of her bulky jacket almost hides her face, but I can see her nose—pink—like she's catching a cold.

"Warm enough?" I ask.

"Yeah," she says.

"So . . . how's it going?"

For the longest time she doesn't answer. At last she

says, "Did you ever feel you were on a train to nowhere and couldn't get off?"

The next breath I take seems to freeze my lungs. "No," I say. "Is that how you feel?"

"Feel . . . felt . . . My whole junior year, down the tube."

"What do you mean? Are you failing? Everything?"

"No. I'll probably pass, but my grades are terrible."

We cross at the corner. "And you haven't talked with a psychologist yet, like your mom suggested?" I ask.

"No. It wouldn't help."

"How can you know that?"

"Because I do," she says. And then, just like before, she flicks the switch and changes the subject. It's like she wants me to know how she feels but doesn't want to discuss why.

So we take the short walk through the trees to the tennis courts, and then we go over to the picnic table. Jodie brushes the leaves off the bench and we sit down, backs against the table.

I tell her about the camera workshop at school. I describe the skateboard sessions in James's garage, and the day at the park in Rockville when I banged myself up good. She asks if I ever talk to James and Luis about her.

"No," I say. I want her to know that everything she tells me is confidential.

"Oh," she says, and I can't tell if she's relieved or disappointed.

Mostly, though, Jodie wants to hear about the coming wedding. "Have you seen her dress?"

"Nope."

"What are her colors?" she asks.

I'll bet there's not a guy in the state of Maryland who, if you said your sister was getting married, would ask what her colors are. She's not a football team. She's not a jockey. But Jodie wants to know, so I say, "Mauve and ivory."

"And what will *you* wear?" she asks.

"Mauve bow tie. Cummerbund. Tux, of course."

"Is she inviting a lot of people?" asks Jodie.

"A hundred and fifty. Something like that."

Jodie wants to know where Marlene and Owen met and how long they've been engaged and where they're going to live. And then suddenly she says she's tired and wants to go home. I figure she's thinking of Gary and wishing things had worked out with him.

She doesn't say much on the way back and doesn't pick up the conversation I throw her way. So after a while I'm quiet too. It feels awkward walking beside Jodie, neither of us talking. We're kicking at the clumps of dead leaves that have fallen on the path—they've frozen in damp clusters, then thawed. She stops to push some aside with the toe of her shoe, to let an early spring flower peep through.

"Do you ever think how the seasons will go right on happening whether we're here or not?" she says. "I mean, after we're gone, we won't be here to see them, but flowers will still keep poking up like this, and summer will still come, just like always."

My feet almost stop moving and my body goes on full alert. Like a computer searching out the right move in a chess game, my mind is desperately trying to find the right response.

"Listen, Jodie," I say. "I know you've been feeling pretty bad lately, and . . . I just want to say that I care about you, so any time you want to talk . . ."

She gives me a quick, almost embarrassed smile, but her eyes well up, so I go on. "You're not alone in this."

"Alone in what?" she asks. And then, sardonically, "Are you serious?" But there's a tremble in her voice.

I can almost see the computer screen in front of me, and I barrel ahead: "When all this is over, I'll still be here and so will you." It's the last thing on the list I can remember, other than *Do you want a hug?*

Jodie doesn't answer. I look over and see that she's crying now. She starts across the next street without even looking.

"Jodie!" I yell, and lunge forward to pull her back, but the oncoming car slams on its brakes and the driver leans on the horn. Jodie gives him the finger and plods on.

The rest of the way home she's crying without making a sound. She turns in at her sidewalk without even saying good-bye.

I reach out and touch her arm. "Jodie, I'm kind of scared for you."

She goes up on her porch and fumbles in her jacket pocket for the key. "Well, don't be," she says, and goes inside.

Once again, Cricket Man loses his chance to save her. Maybe there are just some things he can't handle.

The next few days I mostly see her going in and out of her house, but she never really looks at me, and I can tell she doesn't want to talk. I go over once and ring the doorbell, but when she answers, she doesn't invite me in.

"What do you *want*?" she says irritably.

"I want to know that you're okay."

"I'm *okay*! Quit bugging me!" she says. I give a helpless shrug and leave.

I call her a couple of times, though, when I know she's home, and she only says, "Kenny, just stop calling, all right?" I remember my Cricket Man pledge to save Jodie Poindexter, but what if a person doesn't want to be saved?

I call an 800 hotline number and ask how I can help a girl who is seriously depressed. I can't bring myself to say the other word, though suicide's in the back of my mind. They tell me all the things to say: *I care about you, you're not alone in this, if you need a friend . . . blah, blah, blah.*

Sometimes I get angry. Here I am, wanting to save her

life—wanting to be the one who reaches out to rescue her from the whirlpool—but, like the crickets, she keeps hopping back into the water again. She tells me just enough to make me worry about her, and then she changes the subject.

Then she calls, and I can tell she's been crying. "How are things?" she asks. She's trying to sound normal, but her nose is stopped up. "What are you doing?"

I don't know if I'm more relieved or pissed. It's like I'm on call. "Talking to you," I say. Genius answer.

She sighs. "I just felt like checking in. How's school?"

I can't believe she really wants to know.

"It's okay," I tell her. "How about you?"

She doesn't answer for maybe ten seconds, and I wonder if she's still there. I have the feeling she's crying again. It's hard to take.

"Listen, Jodie, you want me to come over?"

"No," she says. "I just . . . wanted to know you're there."

Now I'm really worried. "I'm here," I say, in as firm and strong a voice as I can. A voice that says, *Lean on me.*

"That's nice to know," she says, so softly I can hardly hear her.

"You *sure* you don't want me to come over?" I ask. Jeez, what if she does something stupid?

"I'm sure," she says, and then she's all business again. Tells me about the history test she flunked and how she's got till Wednesday to make it up, and then she says, "Bye," and that's the end of the phone call.

Jodie Poindexter, you're making me crazy.

The third week of March is cold and blustery. We see Luis running for his bus one day without his Polo jacket. He looks half-frozen. To Luis, anything below fifty degrees is freezing.

"Dude, where's your jacket?" James calls.

Luis looks embarrassed. "Guess I left it somewhere," he calls back, and ducks inside the bus.

"Man, he'd forget his head!" I say. But we shrug it off and head for the bus going to Greyswood.

The next day, though, I don't see Luis in the cafeteria at his usual table with his other seventh-grade friends. I'm sitting by the window across from James, eating my taco, and look out to see Luis backed up against the far fence, three guys around him.

I stop chewing and stare hard.

"Look!" I say.

They're seventh graders too, I think. I recognize one of them, anyway—a heavy kid built like a refrigerator. Luis is standing there in a hoodie, gesturing helplessly, but one of the boys reaches out and grabs him by the collar.

"C'mon," I say, and, leaving our lunch on the table, we head for an exit.

By the time we get around the building and over to the
fence, Luis has taken off one of his Etnies and has handed it
to the big guy. The other two boys are shrimps, wiry little
guys I've seen around school who remind me of weasels.

"Hey!" James yells, running toward them.

The guys turn around and look at him, sneers on their
faces. Then they see me, and the sneers sort of freeze.

"What's up?" I say.

Luis can't speak.

"Give him his shoe back," I say to the refrigerator.

He shrugs and fakes a laugh. "Having a little fun, that's
all," he says, and drops the shoe.

"Yeah," says a weaselly guy. "Just kidding around."

"Yeah?" says James, catching on. "Where's his jacket?"

They look at each other in mock innocence.

"I want his jacket here tomorrow before the bell," I say.
"Understand?"

"Why you telling *us*?" the second weasel protests.

I move over and get right in his face. I'm a foot taller, of
course. "Why do you think?"

"We'll look around," says the refrigerator, starting to slink
away, but James grabs his arm and pulls him back. "What do
you think we ought to do to them?" he asks me, his face hard
as concrete, his voice like gravel. "A nosegrind?"

"Hey, listen," the big guy bleats. "He'll get his jacket,
don't worry."

"And his watch and cell phone," I add. "Tomorrow. Front steps of the school."

The three of them stare at us, then walk away, and we don't say a word till they're out of hearing distance. Then we turn so they can't see the grins on our faces, but Luis is still too scared to grin.

I look at him. "How long's this been going on?"

He's bending over now, tying his shoe. "A while," he mumbles.

"How come you didn't tell us?" asks James.

"They . . . said they'd cut me up good if I told," he says.

"They've got knives?"

He shrugs. "Said they did."

"What'd they take?" I ask.

"Some money. My jacket and stuff."

"Look," I say. "For the rest of the semester, you eat with us, okay?"

He nods his head. "Okay."

The next morning we find his jacket on the school steps, in front of the main entrance. The cell phone and watch were probably sold long ago. *Funkhouser worried about the wrong things back in September*, I'm thinking. Problems aren't always what they seem, and neither are people.

Two weeks before the wedding, the downstairs is filling up with ribbons and bows and shoes and boxes. The weather's on-again, off-again rainy, and I have a choice of staying inside and trying to navigate a path through all the wedding junk or taking my skateboard over to James's and risk running into Nina. I go to the park instead and have a practice session by myself. I stay until the rain gets too heavy to ignore, then head home. When I walk in, I'm about to ask Mom if she'll order carryout for dinner when I hear sobbing coming from the living room.

My first thought is Jodie, but why would she be here? Then I realize it isn't Jodie who's crying, it's my sister.

I take a few steps toward the doorway. Dad and Mom are sitting on the couch across from Marlene, who's in Dad's big chair, hands over her face. Davy's standing just inside the door, and when he sees me, he tiptoes out and comes over.

"What's going on?" I ask.

Davy looks about as confused as I am. "She gave back the ring," he says.

nineteen

I hang around the doorway of the living room, trying to make sense of it all, and when Dad finally gets up and goes out to stand on the porch, Davy and I follow.

"What *happened*?" I ask.

"Marlene just found out that Owen was married." Dad reaches in his shirt pocket for a cigarette, then realizes he's quit. Quit a year ago, actually.

"You mean he didn't get divorced?" asks Davy.

"Of course he's divorced," says Dad.

"Then why is she so upset?" I ask. "It's not bigamy or anything."

"She's upset he didn't tell her—that she had to find out from someone else," says Dad.

"So the wedding's off?" I know it's bad, but this means I won't get Marlene's room.

"That's what your mother's trying to find out," says Dad. And adds, "If it is, there are a hundred and fifty guests to notify, a couple dozen gifts to be sent back, a down payment on the reception that we'll never see again, and a wedding gown to sell on eBay."

"Wow!" says Davy.

"All because he didn't tell her himself?" I say in disbelief.

"Well . . . that's a pretty big thing to keep secret, Kenny," Dad says.

The three of us stand there thinking a minute. "Maybe she should just go ahead and marry him, and *then* if she doesn't like him anymore they could get divorced," says Davy.

Dad looks down at him. "Not the best idea, champ," he says, and gives this big sigh. "No, if they're not right for each other, now's the time to do something about it. I just wish they'd come to this decision three months ago."

The rain's letting up, and the air has the smell of spring. In the glow of the streetlights, I can see the leaf buds shimmering on trees up and down the block. Like the neighborhood's dressed up for something big.

Mom comes out on the porch and leans again Dad. He puts his arm around her, and they just stand there like that for a few minutes.

"I don't know whether to feel sorry for Owen or wring

his neck," Mom says. "Marlene says he's pretty upset."

"Well, so is she, Caroline. She's got a right to be," Dad says.

"I don't even want to think about what's ahead," she says.

"Then don't," says Dad. "It's up to Marlene and Owen to cancel the wedding and tell their guests, not us."

Just don't ask Cricket Man to do it, I'm thinking. At least I'm off the hook as far as the tux and the mauve bow tie.

For the next few days, I don't know whether I'm living in a funeral home or a house for the insane. One minute I hear Marlene crying in the room next to me, and then she's on her cell phone talking to Owen.

"How could you *possibly* think I wouldn't want to know? Now I wonder what *else* you haven't told me . . . ," she's saying.

Two hours later she's asking him the same questions and throws in a whole new set: "Because if you haven't worked out what went wrong in your first marriage, how do I know it won't happen again in ours?"

She's got a point. It gets me wondering why Jodie and Gary broke up. All I know is that Marlene's crying over here and Jodie's miserable across the street, and if this is what happens to people who fall in love, I can wait.

I get my camera and go take some shots on fast film of

those shimmering leaf buds against the streetlights. When I come back into the house, I see the pile of presents in one corner of the dining room, Marlene's bridal veil and tiara tossed on top, and I take a picture of that. From the darkened hallway, I see Mom sitting at the kitchen table, holding a cup of coffee in one hand, resting her chin on the other hand, staring at the wall. *Snap.* Another shot, even though the lighting wasn't that good.

Marlene doesn't go to work the next day. Calls in sick again. Owen calls and Davy answers. Owen says Marlene won't answer her cell phone. Davy tells him that Marlene says she's not home. Owen calls back. Marlene still won't talk to him. Marlene calls Owen. Leaves a message to stop calling.

Marlene won't come to dinner. Mom takes up a tray. Marlene won't eat. Dad suggests we leave her here and the rest of us fly to the Bahamas for a week. Then, when we get back, the whole thing will be decided, one way or another.

"Yes!" says Davy, all excited, and wants to know where the Bahamas are. Mom doesn't think this is funny.

On Wednesday, just after dinner, Marlene's on the phone with her bridesmaids when Owen rings the bell. Marlene looks out her bedroom window and sees his car.

"Don't you dare let him in!" she screams down the stairs.

"Marlene, are you still in high school or will you answer the damn door?" Dad yells back.

She won't come downstairs.

I go to the front door. Owen looks tired, and he's lost a few pounds. His shoulders are stooped, like the weight of his arms is too much for him.

"How you doing?" I say, as though I need to ask.

"I have to see Marlene," he says.

Good for you, Owen, I'm thinking. I stand aside to let him in. "Go on up," I say.

He steps inside and looks hesitantly at Mom and Dad, who are looking hesitantly at him.

"Just go," I say.

Owen starts up the stairs.

"Was that wise?" asks Dad, as Owen's footsteps sound in the hall overhead.

I wait for the shriek.

But all I hear is a door opening. A door closing. When fifteen minutes go by and neither of them comes down, Dad says, "I guess no news is good news." And when an hour goes by and Davy says, "What are they *doing* up there?" Mom suggests I take Davy down to the basement and play a little table tennis, so I do.

When we come up about forty minutes later, Owen and Marlene are sitting together on the couch, and she's wearing his ring again. They're holding hands. Davy and I come to a stop there in the hallway.

Owen's talking: ". . . and I just want to say, with you as witnesses"—he looks at Mom and Dad—"that I won't keep anything like this from Marlene ever again. I just didn't want to ruin my chances with her, and the longer I kept it secret, the more awkward it seemed."

"I wouldn't have been so upset if you'd told me earlier," Marlene says, her thumb stroking the back of his hand.

"But I didn't know that. Now I do." Owen's thumb touches hers. Both thumbs lean toward each other. They bend, touch, stroke. . . . I try not to look.

"Well," says Dad. "Whatever decisions you make are yours alone."

"I appreciate that, Ron," says Owen.

Ron? When did he start calling my dad Ron?

"And the wedding is definitely on," says Marlene.

"Then we have a *lot* to do," says Mom.

I've got homework, so I go upstairs, and Marlene and Owen go out to celebrate their re-engagement. Now that we don't have to notify a hundred and fifty people or sell Marlene's dress on eBay, I can concentrate on other things. But from my desk, where my books and notebooks spill out on the floor and then onto my bed, I can see a light on in Jodie's window across the street. She's not on the roof. I haven't seen Jodie Poindexter on the roof for a long time.

In fact, I don't see much of Jodie at all. Her Toyota comes and goes, but I always seem to miss her, or she manages to miss me. She doesn't return my phone calls, and I don't try anymore. Once in a while I see this friend of hers go up the steps. I feel pretty helpless myself. Angry, too. It's like she's friendly when she needs me, and when she doesn't, I'm a stranger. I'm the one she talks to when she doesn't have anyone else, and Cricket Man's offended. How am I supposed to save someone I never see?

I'm not invited to the bachelor party, but we all survive the rehearsal, the rehearsal dinner, the relatives from out of town, the family photo albums.

The day of the wedding, it looks like it's going to pour. By noon, though, the clouds blow away, the sky clears, and by early afternoon, the sun is out on a perfect April day.

The ceremony's set for four o'clock, but we've had a packed house since eight that morning. The bridesmaids all come over here to get made up and dressed, don't ask me why. We've got two bathrooms upstairs, plus the powder room below. Davy and I have to get up by seven thirty so we'll be out of the way when the girls arrive.

Marlene, of course, has a bunch of cousins and aunts and girlfriends all fussing over her hair. A deli delivers sandwiches and a fruit platter, but I think that Davy and I and Dad are the only ones who eat anything.

I get into my tux around two o'clock just to make sure it fits okay. I'm thinking how I've got about eight more hours of this, and already my collar feels tight. What we don't tell Marlene is that the shop rented the size thirteen patent leather dress loafers I was supposed to get to someone else, and I have to settle for the only other size thirteen shoes in the shop—the standard lace-up kind. And Dad's white fancy shirt is a half size too big at the collar. We figure we can live with this, especially since they gave us 10 percent off the rental price.

Finally the long white limousine pulls up in front of our house, gliding in noiselessly like a cruise ship.

"Wow!" says Davy, running out in his navy blue suit to see inside it. He's disappointed that only the bride and her attendants and Mom get to ride in the limo. He and Dad and I are going in Dad's car.

Some of the neighbors are out on their porches watching as Marlene comes out of the house, the maid of honor holding up the train of Marlene's dress. There isn't anyone out on the Poindexters' porch, though. The Toyota's there, but the other two cars are gone—her folks working weekends, as usual. I would have thought I'd at least see Jodie peeking out the curtains or something, but I don't.

When the limo doors are closed, the driver gets back in, and the limo pulls slowly out into the street on its way to the church.

"Well, guys," Dad says to Davy and me. "Let's go get your sister married. Try to keep that suit clean, Davy. You guys look great."

I figure what Dad doesn't know won't hurt him. After I'd

carried my tux downstairs that morning so the bridesmaids could use my room, I discovered I didn't have a T-shirt, and I sweat a lot when I'm dressed up. But when I went back for a clean one, the girls had already closed my door. So under the rented tuxedo with the white pleated shirt and mauve bow tie, I'm wearing my Cricket Man T-shirt, and I'm hoping the logo won't show through.

twenty

Okay. I've used deodorant. I've used mouthwash. I've cleaned my nails and combed my hair. I'm about as perfect as I can get, and I'm ushering guests to their seats in the church.

"Bride's family or groom's?" I whisper, then walk each guest to the appropriate side of the sanctuary. Is it a contest? I wonder. When the groom stands up there at the altar waiting for his wife-to-be, does he mentally count the rows that are filled on the groom's side of the aisle versus the bride's? When the bride comes down the aisle, do her eyes scan the guests, and does she check to see if the Donaldsons are sitting on the groom's side instead of hers?

I usher Mom to her place in the second row. She's wearing a suit that matches her purse and shoes. Her arm's linked in mine, and she gives it a little squeeze when I let her go. Owen's mom leans forward and smiles at Mom across the aisle.

Now the music's getting louder, and I'm standing up near Owen at the altar with the best man and the other three ushers. We're turned a little toward the back of the sanctuary, our spines stiff, arms relaxed, hands clasped in front of us as though we might be attacked by the brides-maids or something.

And then, here they come: the first of the bridesmaids, from shortest to tallest, the shortest, of course, to be paired with me, even though I'm as big as the usher next to me. I've got to escort her back up the aisle when the ceremony's over and dance with her once at the reception, Marlene says. Man, I hate weddings.

"It's only two minutes, Kenny!" Marlene said when I told her I didn't want to dance with anyone. "That's two minutes for me out of your whole life. Is that too much to ask?"

It is for someone who can't dance. She forgot to men-tion the dress rehearsal, the tux, the starched shirt with the ruffle down the front, the bow tie, the cummerbund, the boutonniere, and an entire day I could have been at the skate park with James and Luis.

But she's my sister, and I get her room when she moves out, so I do my best. I smile when Marlene, looking bet-ter than she'll ever look again in her whole life, probably, comes down the aisle on Dad's arm. He kisses her on the cheek and turns around to sit with Mom, and finally we're getting started.

It's a traditional ceremony, all but the parts Marlene and Owen wrote themselves. Owen faces Marlene and takes her hands and vows that they will live a life without secrets, and Marlene replies that she will trust him always, which maybe tells us a little more than we need to know. And when the minister asks if anyone knows why these two should not be united in holy wedlock, I shift my eyes toward the pews behind me, half expecting Owen's ex-wife to appear and say she never signed the divorce papers.

But nobody objects, Owen and Marlene are pronounced husband and wife, and though their kiss is a bit longer than necessary, the organ peals out the "Wedding March" and we head back up the aisle, the shortest bridesmaid clinging to my arm. Outside, I gulp in the spring air, loosen my collar, and take off my jacket for a minute so I can cool off.

Davy comes out with Mom and Dad, who are greeting guests.

"Let's never do this again," I tell Davy. "I'm going to get married in a skate park."

Davy laughs. "*I'm* going to get married jumping out of an airplane!" he says.

We go back inside for what feels like hours of wedding pictures. Then we're at the reception and everybody smiles while Marlene and Owen dance together. Then Dad dances with Marlene, and Owen dances with his mom. Then all the ushers and bridesmaids dance, and I don't do so bad after all. Finally . . . *finally* . . . we get to eat.

There are toasts to the bride and groom, more dancing and laughing, and, of course, the cutting of the cake. About nine o'clock, I've had enough. I've been wearing the tux since two, and my feet hurt.

Mom comes to the rescue.

"Kenny," she says, "the Millers are leaving, and they've offered to take some of the wedding presents home in their car. Do you want to ride along and open the door for them, or would you rather stay here?"

Is this a trick question? "Do I have to come back?" I ask.

"No, honey. Just unlock the door and help them carry the gifts inside. Davy wants to stay a little longer. He likes the band."

"Sure, no problem," I say, and we get a luggage cart from the front desk and put all the presents on it. Then we wheel it out to our neighbors' car.

You'd think people would know that they're not supposed to carry gifts to a reception. Why do they think the bride's family wants to carry the presents back to the house when that's where they should have been delivered in the first place? But it gives me an excuse to leave, so I don't complain.

The Millers live a couple of doors down from us, and

they're in the front seat while I'm in the back beside a tower of boxes, a few more on my lap.

"You okay back there?" Mr. Miller asks jovially, checking the rearview mirror. "If any of those boxes start to fall, just holler."

"I'm okay."

"Wasn't that a lovely wedding?" says Mrs. Miller. "Goodness! Marlene looked so beautiful. I can't believe she's the same girl who used to sunbathe right on the front lawn!"

"I think you're thinking of that girl across the street— the Poindexters' daughter," Mr. Miller says.

"Oh my, I can't keep track of everyone," Mrs. Miller says. "So many people moving in and out. Your family moved in the fall before last, didn't you?" she asks me over her shoulder.

"That's right," I say.

"Well, we never seem able to spend as much time with our neighbors as we'd like, but your mother and I go to the book discussions at the library, Kenny, and I've certainly enjoyed her company."

Mr. Miller backs his Cadillac into our driveway and I get out, unlock the front door, and help bring the presents inside. One load, two . . . Mrs. Miller comes in on the last trip, mostly, I think, to see what our house looks like inside. Her husband just says, "Where do you want these?" while Mrs. Miller's checking out the furniture.

"Thanks a lot," I say. "I know Mom and Dad appreciate it."

"A neighbor did the same for us when our daughter got married," Mrs. Miller says. And with a final look around, she adds, "I know how long it takes to get back to normal after a wedding."

We say good night and they leave. I'm wondering which I want most—to get out of this tux or eat one of the leftover gourmet sandwiches the deli delivered that morning.

The sandwich wins out, and I unwrap a ham and cheese on a croissant. I don't even get the first bite, though, before the phone rings.

I pick it up in the kitchen. "Hello?"

At first I don't hear anything. Then I hear crying. *Not Marlene again!* I'm thinking. Don't tell me Owen had another confession to make.

"Who's this?" I keep saying. "Hello? Hello . . . ?"

And then a voice says, "Kenny . . ." More crying. "I've been calling and calling. . . ."

"Jodie? *Jodie?*" I say quickly. "What's the matter? Where are you?"

"Please help me," she says. "I'm at the picnic table . . . at the park . . . *Please.* As soon as you can . . ."

And I'm running like a maniac in my tux and my rented shoes. All Cricket Man wants is to get there in time.

twenty-one

She probably didn't *try to shoot herself*, I'm thinking as I skid along in my rented shoes with the slick soles. *Cut her wrists, maybe?* I should have warned her parents. Should have brought bandages, a blanket. My cell phone, at least.

A car honks at me as I race across the road, then the parking lot, and head for the trees. It's dark under there, and I'm only guessing at the path. A branch with thorns grabs at my sleeve, and I feel it snag as I jerk myself free. I wonder if the tux will be returnable. . . .

At least she isn't dead, I tell myself. If she'd really wanted to kill herself, she would have done it right. She wouldn't have called. Sometimes, I've read, a suicide attempt is just a call for help.

The trees are thinning out and I'm nearing the tennis

courts. The moon's three-quarters full, so there's some light, but not a lot.

I'm out of breath, running along the path, heading over to the small playground and the picnic table beyond. Past the dead-end road where James and Luis and I practice our tricks.

I can see someone there at the table—*on* the table, actually—and as I get closer, I can hear Jodie crying softly.

"Jodie?" I'm calling. "Jodie?"

I can't tell if she's sitting up or lying down, but her knees are bent. And between her legs, on the picnic table, is a baby.

I can't seem to move or speak. My nose picks up the scent of blood, of birth.

"Help me," Jodie cries, and her voice sounds like a kitten's mew.

I stare at her stupidly and feel my own blood draining from my face. "What's happened?"

"What do you *think*?" she cries.

I take a few steps closer. In the moonlight, I see that Jodie's got nail scissors or something and is snipping away at the umbilical cord.

"Jodie!" I say. "Is it okay?" But then its legs and arms move and it cries: *"Wha . . . ah . . . ah . . . ah . . ."* When I get right up to the picnic table, I see it's a boy, and he's covered with some kind of white stuff and blood. The whole place is a mess.

Jodie's crying harder, now that I'm here, and she wipes her nose on her arm. There's a towel beneath her, and on it is a dark red mass beside the baby. The cord goes from the baby to this blob of whatever it is. I never felt so helpless.

"Have you got anything to tie the cord with?" Jodie weeps.

I stare. "Are we supposed to do this?" I ask, my voice quavery. "W-where do I tie it?"

"I don't know!" she cries. "Just help me!"

I reach down and untie the black lace on one of my patent leather shoes. My hands are shaking.

The scissors finally cut through the cord and the two ends bleed a little. Jodie lies back on the table, her knees together now, and pulls the edge of her coat over her, looking exhausted.

I don't even know what to begin to ask. I'm tying a shoelace around the end of a cord attached to a baby. He's lying there on the edge of the towel, his small bare body trembling as he wails, and Jodie's not even looking at him.

"Why did you come out here?" I ask her. "Jodie, what were you *thinking*?"

"I . . . I couldn't have the baby at home. Mom and Dad would be coming . . . and . . . I was on my way to Sara's," she says.

I don't get it.

"She's coming back from a movie tonight, but . . . but

I figured I could make it to their porch. They've got a back porch. . . ." Her voice fades away in fatigue.

"She knows?"

"She s-suspects, maybe," Jodie says, and now she's crying again.

The baby's arms are flailing, and he's crying louder now. Jodie puts her hands over her ears.

"Take it," she says.

"What?"

"*Take* it," she says, almost angrily.

"*Where?*"

"I don't know! I don't care, but don't take it home!" she sobs. "Just *go!*"

I feel like I'm freezing inside. Then I'm burning up. "Jodie, it's your *baby!*" I tell her, as if she didn't know. As if she thought it was a melon, maybe.

"I don't want it," she weeps. And then she hisses, "Just take it somewhere. *Anywhere!* And don't bring it back."

I can't believe this is happening. Can't believe what she's saying. Is she asking me to abandon it somewhere? It's chilly. How long can a newborn baby survive without a blanket?

I take off my tuxedo jacket, spread it out on the picnic table, and gently pick up the baby. He's got wrinkles above his nose. I place his warm, slippery body on it, then wrap it around him and pick him up, holding him against me. He's so small.

I study Jodie there on the table, pulling her clothes on.

"I can't leave you, Jodie," I say. "I can't leave you here like this."

"I'm okay," she insists.

"But . . . the blood!"

"It's *okay*. Now go!"

I remember a picture of the tribal woman in *National Geographic*, returning to the fields two hours after having a baby. What do I know about this stuff?

"Okay, but I'll be right back," I say, and set off toward Democracy Boulevard.

"Don't tell *anyone*!" Jodie calls after me. "Promise!"

I'm breathing so hard it's like I'm breathing for both of us. The baby seems to weigh almost nothing in my arms, but every so often he gives this shaky little cry—"*Wah . . . ah . . . ah . . . ah . . . ah*"—like he hasn't quite figured out how to do it. I can't run because the shoe without the lace is loose on my foot, and it goes *thwap, thwap* as I walk.

How could I have missed the pregnancy? *How?* This isn't a Cricket Man moment any longer. This time it's real. I'm holding a live baby in my arms, and I'm scared.

I'm coming to the fire station from the back. Out on Democracy the cars are zooming by, the usual Saturday night traffic going to and from the mall. The baby cries again, and his tiny body shakes with the effort. I think how this is the most important night of his whole life, and his mom's giving him away. I'm numb.

I walk around to the front of the station. The truck doors are open to the sweet night air. Three firemen are sitting on folding chairs just inside by one of the trucks. They're drinking coffee, laughing and joking with one another. Then they see me.

The smiles disappear from their faces.

"Holy shit!" one of them murmurs. They spring from their chairs, their eyes traveling down my body. I realize that the front of my shirt and my hands are smeared with blood.

"Buddy, you okay?" one of them says, coming forward. And then he hears the baby.

"Please, take him," I say, and hand the baby over.

He stares at the baby, at me, eyes wide. They all stare.

"It's a boy," I say, and figure they'll call the police. My head is about to explode.

"Uh . . . hold on there, son," the second man says. "You want to give us your name?"

Do I *want* to give them my name? I've got a choice? I shake my head.

"Okay, okay. Just tell us this: Is the mother all right?" asks the third man.

I start backing away. "I . . . I think so," I say. "Yes."

"Is there anything we can do to help? Anyone you want us to call?" asks the man with the baby.

I shake my head. And then I run, leaving my bloody tuxedo jacket with them.

Any minute I expect to be tackled. I'm not running very fast because of my stupid shoe. I expect a searchlight to be turned in my direction. To hear the sound of footsteps behind me. But that doesn't happen. Nobody calls after me. Nobody comes.

When I get to the picnic table, Jodie's gone, and so is the towel. There's some blood on the table and a little on one of the benches.

"Jodie?" I call out. *"Jodie?"*

No answer.

I start back toward the tennis courts, then the trees. I don't know where her friend Sara lives. All I can do is go home. My eyes are like radar, though, scanning the path to see if Jodie's crumpled up in the brush somewhere. Do I want her to suffer a little, leaving her baby like that? I've got a million questions, but she probably won't answer any of them.

I'm exhausted now. I reach the street and let a whole string of cars go by before I even try to cross. A couple of them slow, and someone leans out a window to ask if I'm all right. I just wave him on.

As I go up our street, I see Jodie on her front steps, between her parents, who are helping her into the house. I figure she was trying to get home first and clean up a little before they got there. Didn't work, and I'm glad. Glad *some-one's* in on this now besides me. I watch for a minute, then take my key and open our front door.

Mom and Dad and Davy are already back.

They haven't been home long, because Dad's still got his jacket on, and Mom's in her high-heeled shoes. They're standing in the dining room, exclaiming over the pile of wedding gifts stacked against one wall.

"Man!" Davy's saying. "It's like Christmas! It'll take them a whole *year* to open all those!"

And then they turn and see me. Mom gives a little scream.

"Kenny! What happened?" Dad asks. "Were you in a fight?"

I shake my head and go into the kitchen. Take off my white shirt and drop it in the sink. I'm standing there in my Cricket Man T-shirt and my tuxedo pants and my shoes with one lace missing. Then I see there's blood on the T-shirt.

"The Cr—The T-shirt!" Danny cries. He stares at me.

I take that off too and drop it on the floor.

Mom keeps saying, "What happened? Kenny, what happened?"

"I'm really tired," I say. "Please. I've got to take a shower. I'll tell you later."

"KENNY!" Dad shouts, starting toward me. "I want answers here. Are you *hurt*?"

"No!" I yell, and my voice cracks. "There wasn't any fight and nobody's hurt! Please! Let me get a shower and then we'll talk." I realize my eyes are wet. Am I almost *crying? Jeez!*

Dad stops, considering, then looks at Mom, and I go upstairs.

In the bathroom, I strip down and stand unmoving, exhausted, drained, under the hot spray. I guess I'm asking a lot of them. Dad trusted what I told him when the police followed me home; Mom tried to respect my privacy after Funkhouser called. They're trusting me now. How can I not tell them about the baby? How am I supposed to explain the blood on my hands, my clothes? Jodie's parents have to know by now, but what if they *don't?* What if Jodie makes up some other kind of story?

I replay the evening in my head. The last six months. How could I not have noticed? But then, no one else did either. Jodie was definitely depressed, but there was so much more for her to worry about. My mind goes back to the girl on the porch roof, head on her arms. Jodie in the old sweat suit. Jodie in the bathrobe . . .

When I've used all the hot water, I dry off, pull on an old pair of jeans, and go downstairs for the rest of my clothes. The tuxedo jacket's done for, but I figure I can at least soak the shirt in a pail of water.

I start through the hallway to the kitchen and see Davy

sitting stiffly on a chair. Mom and Dad are standing over him, and I hear Dad say, "I don't care *what* you promised, Davy! What does it *stand* for?" And he's holding my Cricket Man T-shirt.

Davy doesn't answer. Tears are running down his cheeks.

I step into the kitchen.

"Cricket Man," I say, and take the shirt. "The 'CM' stands for Cricket Man."

Davy stops crying and stares at me. Dad's face goes blank. Mom looks puzzled. I'm sick of secrets, but I'm not angry anymore. I'm tired.

"It was just a logo I thought up for rescuing crickets and things in the pool last summer. Just a little thing going between Davy and me that got out of hand when Funkhouser jumped on it at school."

Mom sits down slowly. "That's *all*?"

"That's all."

"Then why didn't you tell Mr. Funkhouser when he asked?" she wants to know.

"Because I didn't think I should have to," I say. "And I didn't want it to get around school."

"It doesn't have anything to do with tonight?"

"No."

"What *did* happen tonight?" Dad asks.

I sit down heavily on a kitchen chair. "Davy," I say,

"I've got to talk to Mom and Dad. In private, okay?"

He doesn't want to go, obviously.

"And hey, listen. Thanks for covering for me." I give his arm a squeeze. "You're the best."

"Go on up to your room, Davy," Mom says. "We'll be up after a while."

"Can I take a Jacuzzi?" he asks. Big treat at our house.

"Yes," she says. "But fill the tub before you turn it on."

Davy heads for the stairs, and when I hear his shoes thump on the floor above, I turn to my parents. "When I got home from the reception, Jodie called. She told me to come to the park, and when I got there, she'd had a baby."

Mom and Dad stare at me without blinking. Mom's lips mouth *What?* but no sound comes out.

"A *baby?*" asks Dad.

"She'd given birth on a picnic table and needed help with the cord."

"My . . . *God!*" breathes Mom, one hand to her face. "Is it . . . is she . . . all right?"

"I think so," I say. "She's home now, and her parents are there, but I don't know if she's told them about the baby or not. It was a boy, and I took him to the fire station."

"The *fire* station?" asks Dad, bewildered.

I nod. "She didn't want him. Told me just to take him away. Anywhere."

Like me, my parents don't know where to begin. The

air is so heavy with questions you can almost feel them pushing up against your face. But before they can start, the doorbell rings and Dad answers.

I hear Mr. Poindexter say, "Ron, I need to talk to Kenny."

He comes out in the kitchen, looking really old, not that I've seen him that much. He glances at my family, then focuses on me.

"I've just got two questions, Kenny," he says. "Where is it, and is it yours?"

twenty-two

Shock.

"What?" Since I could never imagine Jodie Poindexter feeling romantic toward me, I couldn't imagine anyone even remotely suspecting the baby was mine.

"Which of those questions don't you understand?" Mr. Poindexter snaps.

"Kenny, he's asking if you're the father," Mom says gently, zombielike.

"Hell, no! God, no! Of course not!"

Jodie's dad is suddenly embarrassed. "I'm sorry," he says. He closes his eyes for a second and runs one hand across his forehead. "This has been a very upsetting night." He puts his other hand on the back of a chair and leans on it. "Jodie would only say she gave the baby to you. Where is it?"

The baby's still an "it."

"I took him to the firehouse on Democracy."

"A boy? Then it ... he ... was alive?" Mr. Poindexter asks, and I see his eyes glisten.

"Yeah. He was crying. Moving. He seemed to be breathing okay. I wrapped him up in my jacket," I say.

"Ed, don't you want to sit down?" Mom offers. "We could go into the living room. ..."

"I'm okay, thanks," Mr. Poindexter says, and pulls out the kitchen chair. He sits down. So does Dad.

"How long have you known that Jodie was pregnant?" her dad asks.

"I didn't know it at all until tonight, when she called me from the park," I say. "She was on her way to a friend's house to have the baby there."

Mr. Poindexter shakes his head. "I still can't believe it. She went through this all alone. She might have died. Ellen's terribly upset."

"I think she figured she could make it to Sara's, but she didn't," I say, trying to explain someone's actions when I can't even understand them myself. I can't even understand how a baby can get *out* of a mother, when you come right down to it.

"Kenny, how did you cut the umbilical cord?" asks Mom.

"Jodie used nail scissors," I tell her.

They all stare at me. "How did you *tie* it?" asks Dad.

"With my shoelace," I say. "We'll probably get charged for that when we take those shoes back. That and the jacket." I don't realize how ridiculous it sounds till the words are out.

"And the placenta?" asks Mom.

Come on! I'm thinking. *I'm not an obstetrician.* "Something was there on the towel beside the baby. Maybe that was it."

Nobody says anything. The adults just stare at one another. We can hear the whirlpool going upstairs, but other than that, the house is silent.

Mr. Poindexter exhales. "It's unbelievable that we didn't know," he says. "You hear about this happening in other families, but . . ." His voice fades for a moment. "We knew something was wrong, but we figured it all had to do with her breakup with the boyfriend. Ellen wanted her to talk to a psychologist, but Jodie wouldn't go. We didn't push it. We figured things would work themselves out."

"Well, they generally do," says Mom. "But the important thing is that Jodie's okay."

"Yes, we're glad of that." Mr. Poindexter looks at me again. "Is Gary the father, do you know? Her old boyfriend?"

I shake my head. "You'd have to get that from Jodie."

He's nodding even before I finish, and lets out his breath. "Right. Can we assume that what happened tonight is confidential? I'd really appreciate it if it didn't go further than this room."

"Of course," says Dad.

"If anyone talks about it, it will have to be Jodie," I say.

"Now," Mr. Poindexter says, standing, "I want to see my grandson. And . . . thank you, Kenny."

Dad walks him to the door. When he comes back to the kitchen, he puts an arm around me and says, "Kenny, that was a good thing you did."

"What?"

"The fire station. How'd you think of that?"

I don't know what he means. "What else could I do? I figured they'd know what to do for a new baby. I was afraid they'd call the police or something, all the blood, but I did it anyway."

"In Maryland, parents can turn over a newborn baby to a hospital or rescue squad and they don't have to identify themselves," says Mom. "Just . . . just give it away."

"But I'm not the father!" I say.

"Well, the firemen didn't know that," she says. "I'm curious. What *did* they say when they saw you with the baby?"

"They asked if I wanted to give my name. I said no. They asked if the mother was okay. I said yes. Then I came home."

"You did everything right," Dad says.

We talk for another half hour, and then we're talked out. For now, anyway.

"I'm exhausted," Dad says. "It's been a crazy day. I'm going up to tuck Davy in. Then I'm going to bed."

"I've got to unwind," says Mom. "Tomorrow, let's just take it easy all day. Let's not do anything we don't absolutely have to."

"I'm all for that," Dad says, and heads for the stairs.

Mom goes out on the back porch to sit on the glider in the dark, and I follow her. It's a mild April night—the kind of night that Cricket Man might have been out on the roof, watching for Jodie. We sit quietly for a while, pushing with our feet against the floor, and finally Mom says, "It's hard being a parent. It's the hardest job in the world."

I don't say anything, sorry for the worry I've caused her.

"I'm sorry we badgered Davy about your T-shirt. He was trying so hard to be loyal to you. I'm sorry I badgered *you*."

Now there's sorry all over the place.

"I should have told you sooner," I mumble. "It was just a fun little thing we had going. I figured it would sound stupid to anyone else but Davy. And then . . . it just got bigger and bigger. . . ."

Mom doesn't reply to that. Instead she says, "I wonder what they'll do about the baby if Jodie doesn't want to keep him. I can't imagine ever giving up a baby."

"I can't ever imagine being Jodie," I say. "Maybe if I could, I'd understand."

"That's true," says Mom. "And the Poindexters will probably spend the rest of their lives wondering how they failed Jodie."

"I don't get it," I say. "Jodie gets pregnant and somehow it's *their* fault?"

"Ah, Kenny, that's the way it goes," says Mom. "Parents spend a good chunk of their lives regretting either what they did or could have done. Even when we manage to do things right, we always think of ways we could have done it better."

"Well, *that* sucks!" I say, and she laughs. "Seriously, I think you're doing a good job, Mom. Yeah, you badgered some, but you also respected me even when you didn't quite trust me, and that's huge."

She reaches over and pats my thigh.

"Sometimes you manage to say exactly the right thing at the right moment, you know that?"

Cricket Man comes through again. And I'm not even wearing the shirt.

twenty-three

I don't see Jodie the next couple of days. On Thursday, though, when I know her parents are gone, I ring the bell.

I see the curtain move as she peeks out. There's a pause, but finally the door opens. She looks about the same, but the puffiness has gone from her face.

"Hey, Kenny. Come on in," she says.

I listen for the sound of a baby in the background, but I don't hear anything. After everything that happened, how can she still look the same? But she does. A girl's body is a mystery to me. Life is a mystery.

"How you doing?" I ask. "*Really.*"

She pauses. "I've been meaning to call you," she says.

Meaning to call? Are we back to that on-again, off-again deal? "So are you okay or not?" I ask.

"Yes. I'm okay. Thanks for taking care of things."

"It wasn't a 'thing,' Jodie. It was a baby."

"I know," she says.

I follow her into the living room. She's been eating a bowl of ice cream. She holds out the spoon. "Want some?"

"No, thanks." I sit across from her, and she puts the bowl back down.

"The doctor says I'm fine, and I'm going back to school next week."

"That's good."

"Uh-huh," she says, but she looks distracted, then anxious. "Listen, Kenny. When my father went over to your place, did he give you a hard time? I've wanted to ask."

"Not really. He was just upset. Wanted to know if I was the father."

It's the first time I've seen Jodie blush. "God! Sorry, Kenny. I finally had to tell them it's Gary's. Not that it matters. I mean, if I'd kept the baby, I would have asked the jerk for child support, but I don't want anything to do with him—anything that would *remind* me of him."

She's not keeping the baby, then. "Does Gary know?" I ask.

"About the baby?" She nods. "Yeah, he knows. If he can count, he can figure about when it was due. I haven't told him yet that I delivered." Jodie picks up a sofa pillow and props it behind her head, slides down a little, and rests her feet on the coffee table. Her eyes avoid mine. "He used to tell me he loved me all the time. We even talked about getting married some day. Having children! And you know what he said when I told him I might be pregnant? 'How could you be so stupid?' His exact words."

"You must have felt pretty bad," I say.

"I was even stupider than stupid," she goes on. "We argued for two days, and then we broke up. But I still didn't believe he meant it. I figured he was in shock, and that once he realized it was the baby we'd talked about having—*our* baby—he'd love me even more, and we'd figure out what to do.

"For the first month or so, he'd call, then he wouldn't. We'd talk, then we wouldn't. Sometimes he sounded so sweet, and I'd think everything was going to be okay. Then . . . he stopped calling at all. I think I was numb. I know it's crazy, but I really thought I'd have a miscarriage. I was *sure* I'd have one, because I didn't look pregnant at all. I figured something was probably wrong with the baby. Then . . . about the seventh month . . . it began to sink in that maybe I was wrong."

"But why didn't you tell your parents?" I ask.

"Because by then it was too late for an abortion, and I knew they'd go insane. They've just opened this law office in DC, and they work all the time. They don't even have time for me. They wouldn't know what to do if they had a grandchild."

"They could change," I say.

Jodie shakes her head. "You don't know them. Anyway, it's over. I'm not keeping the baby. They're upset with me, but I think they're relieved, in a way. They've both seen him, but they don't have time to raise him either."

I don't say anything.

"Do *you* think I should have kept him?" she asks.

"No," I say. "I think a kid needs to come into the world with as many things going for him as possible."

She nods. "That's the way I feel. I didn't want to see him because I might have wanted to keep him. I'm really not ready to be a mother, Kenny. There are all these couples out there who want a baby so much. We're starting family therapy, though. The doctor suggested it." Jodie laughs a little. "She made it sound like if we didn't start family therapy, I might get pregnant again. So it's like therapy as birth control."

If someone had told me six months ago that come spring I'd be sitting with Jodie Poindexter discussing birth control, I'd have said, *What the heck are you smoking, anyway?*

I laugh. "Whatever. I'm glad you're going back to school."

"Yeah. And here's something I've decided: If anybody asks why I was out, I'm going to tell them the truth."

I'm surprised, but I try not to show it.

"Mom's totally against it. She says it'll mark me for life.

I say I'm already marked. You can't go through something like this without being changed in some way. I didn't keep the baby, but I don't want to hide the fact that I had it. *Him*, I mean. I'm done with secrets. And it was hardest of all keeping it from you."

"Me? How come?"

"Because you were the one person who listened."

I shake my head. "Maybe I was the only person you talked to," I say, and she smiles.

"Maybe that, too," she says. "But you give off this sort of . . . energy, you know? And I guess I hoped some would rub off on me."

I give this incredulous laugh. "What?"

"You just always look like you're going places, doing things. Maybe it's the skateboard, I don't know. Like you're this huge, supercharged battery . . ."

"Not the Energizer Bunny," I say.

"No, way more than that." She smiles at me again, a warm smile, and I smile back.

We talk about school then, and I tell her about the camera workshop. Ask if she'd ever let me take her picture for my portraiture assignment.

"Like where? Right here?"

"Anywhere you want. On the roof, even."

She laughs. "I'll think about it."

When I get up to leave, Jodie's still sitting on the couch,

cross-legged now. She stretches out her arm and extends her index finger.

"Touch."

I look puzzled.

"When I was about nine," she says. "I went through this obsessive-compulsive phase where I had to touch every-thing twice. I imagined my touch was a little person I was leaving behind that no one else could see. But I didn't want to leave him alone, so if I touched the top of my dresser, I had to touch it again. If I touched a doorknob, I'd do it again." She was still holding her arm out.

I reach over, extending my arm, my index finger, and lightly touch the tip of hers.

Jokingly, she jerks back like something sparked. "Yep," she says. "There's a charge, all right." She touches my finger again and grins.

That Sunday I take my board over to James's, where he and Luis are doing a little practice. I never told them about the baby because I never told them about Jodie. I never told them about Jodie because they'd never believe we were just friends.

James and Luis are on the steps, skateboards on their laps, putting new grip tape on the decks. They peel off the backing and stick it to the surface, then razor the excess away.

I tell them I want to take their picture sometime at the skate park—an action shot for the camera workshop. James puts down his board, steps on with one foot, extends the other leg out behind him, and spreads his arms like a skater on ice, and we laugh.

"Seriously, though, I want the picture to say something. What it really means when you're skating."

James picks up his board again and tightens the trucks. "Freedom," he says. "On a board, you're flying. Doing something you never thought you could do."

I know the feeling.

The door from the house opens and Nina comes out.

"I *thought* I heard you," she says, and smiles flirtatiously at me.

"Nursery school!" James declares. "Bring out the orange juice."

"If you want me to leave, why don't you just say so?" Nina tells him.

"So leave," James says. He rolls across the garage, goes up the ramp, does a 180, and comes back down.

Nina turns to Luis and me. "What about you?" she asks.

Luis shrugs. He doesn't talk to girls unless it's a matter of life or death.

She turns to me. "Kenny? Leave or stay?"

I look at Nina looking at me, braced for rejection. The

guys are looking at me. If this was Jodie, I'd say something to make her laugh. But Nina needs—deserves—something more than a laugh.

"Leave," I say, "but I'll save you a seat."

"What?" she asks.

I grin. "Camera workshop tomorrow. I'll even take your picture."

"O-*kay!*" she says, surprised. Pleased. And gives me a 100 percent natural, organic, no-artificial-sweeteners smile.

I pick up my board and practice my kickflips.

Jodie calls me that evening.

"Well, I did it," she says.

"Yeah? Did what?"

"I went over to Sara's and told her everything. Then we called Jessica and Pat and Kelly and Lisa and I told them, too. I decided I can't put the past behind me if I know people are talking behind my back. And there's nothing to gossip about if I'm the one who's talking."

"You're really cool, Jodie," I say, like I've known her all my life. "Nice going!"

I climb out on the porch roof that night—out Marlene's window, now that I've taken over her room—and sit with my back against the house, listening to traffic over on Democracy Boulevard, searching for stars.

I'm thinking about going to the skate park next week-end and taking a dozen shots of James doing a switch half-flip above a six-stair rail. About buying a board for Davy on his birthday and giving him lessons. About checking out that book I saw at the library—*The Book of Photography* from National Geographic.

It will soon be May, and in June we'll open our pool. Mom will be taking her last summer course at the university, which means I'll get up early to look after things while she's gone. I'll go out to the pool in the early morning and turn on the filter. Slide into the water at the shallow end and start my rescue operation. The lightning bugs, the June bugs, a grasshopper or two, and especially the crickets will go on jumping right back in again, same as before. But I'll go on saving them, same as before, because some of them—a few, anyway—will take a new direction.